Praise for *Gigantic:*

"A staunch enemy of cliché, Nesbitt has attempted to tweak his imagery and metaphors in unpredictable ways."
—David Massengill, *Seattle Weekly*

"The push-pull struggle between the narrators and those who wield power combines with Nesbitt's snappy command of language to create stories with real depth."
—Heather Lee Schroeder, *Capital Times*

"Driven by hard, explosive prose, an almost insane ability to coil metaphors, and endings so shockingly nimble they'll send you back to the beginnings to start again."
—Kaelen Wilson-Goldie, *Black Book*

"Nesbitt seems to have sprung, fully formed, from out of nowhere. His language is rich and brutal enough to knock the wind out of you."
—*Contents*

"This clever, raucous debut collection . . . offers ten stories that explore a hard, racially charged world, bitterness and compassion vying for top billing. . . . Nesbitt's idiosyncratic voice, his sharp-tongued observations and his convincing, colloquial dialogue communicate a unique and arresting worldview."
—*Publishers Weekly*

"*Gigantic* is a brilliant collection of stories. Marc Nesbitt sees life in all its dark possibility without letting go of an essential humanity, and he gives this vision a stunningly eloquent voice. We need to listen to him."
—Robert Olen Butler

GIGANTIC

GIGANTIC

STORIES

Marc Nesbitt

Grove Press
New York

Published simultaneously in Canada
Printed in the United States of America

FIRST PAPERBACK EDITION

Library of Congress Cataloging-in-Publication Data

Nesbitt, Marc.
      Gigantic : stories / Marc Nesbitt.
          p. cm.
      ISBN 0-8021-3963-9 (pbk.)
      1. United States—Social life and customs—20th century—Fiction. I. Title.
PS3614.E49 G5 2002
813'.6—dc21   2001040707

Grove Press
841 Broadway
New York, NY 10003

03 04 05 06 07   10 9 8 7 6 5 4 3 2 1

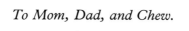

To Mom, Dad, and Chew.

CONTENTS

Maybe I could hide out here but who's looking for me.
Jim Harrison, *A Good Day to Die*

The Ones Who May Kill You in the Morning

ME AND CAPTAIN EARL STAND WHERE THE LAWN ENDS, EACH with a side of driveway and a lantern to hold. Two black guys they dress up as jockeys: I get the checkered shirt, red and cream, number 13, helmet tight like a nutshell and pants skim as a James Brown dancer. Captain Earl in vertical blue and white stripes but you can't see the number from here. His tights fit worse than mine. No matter what color suit, your gloves are always white.

An hour already with nothing to stare at but crab apples in the gravel. This is the road the wealthy live on— just gray rocks dead in their own dust, running past us, in front of us, winding through the woods. Between the crab trees scabbed birch trunks zigzag, unsure where to twist. Our lights burn like fists.

"Even the rich road's nothing but stones," I say, like a fortune cookie.

Luckily, Earl can't hear me because of headphones he welded into his helmet. He's at least fifty, eldest and head of the lawn jockeys, or "Captain," I should call him, because "We're all a team," the people who own the house told me.

My left shoulder's swollen twice the size of my right. Wind in the trees, and the leaves show us their backsides. Soon they'll all be dead. I turn and face the house, sit on my lantern.

If I sprinted the whole way, I could cross this guy's lawn in three days easy. I heard his flat grass had bored him so he hired Asian landscapers to make it undulate—had to be Asian. *You seen them bonsai trees?* he'd said. Now he's got a sod wave-pool four football fields long for his lawn, bending in the ripples as if the house had dropped on it. The driveway crosses the tops of the waves, and they bricked in the dips beneath it.

A herd of oaks explode from here to the house. Their mass grows as you notice them—just now rammed up through the earth, shaking with size, limbs dripping dirt. Their shadows lie long at their sides. White holiday lights come alive among the branches, large as gargoyles to shine on those below. Cold piles toward nightfall. It's six o'clock late September, second night of work.

First day was an afternoon picnic. Caterers dropped from the backs of black minivans like Airborne, moving in formation, advancing on the backyard. Instead of lanterns, jockeys hold black iron rings in the day. They gave me a wet one, so dark I could see myself in it. When I didn't grab the ring, the guy handing them out said, "Make your glove dirty just looking at it, don't it?" Light-blue kid with hair like a pride of fire ants. He was the kid of something famous, and by now nobody knew either one of them. I saw him again after all the food was gone, holding a mints bowl by the sidewalk where everyone left.

With the last guest and the redhead gone, I cleaned up all their shit and burned the butter-plaid tablecloths.

"You can't just throw them away," a skinny big man said, so tall his knees needed bolts and he stooped wherever he went, not just through doorways but there in the backyard daylight, saving his scalp from the bare bulb sun on its low string. "You gotta burn them."

He'd pointed to a dumpster with Hell in it, where the rest of The Help cradled bundles and already lined toward the fire.

But tonight's Ruffhauser, a German chef with his name italicized on the invite, so the linen'll stay on the table. Somebody posted an invite in the locker room; the menu half ripped off, neat along the card fold so The Help couldn't even see what the food tastes like.

The first car shows up smoking stone at the wheels. Dead leaves jump in the headlights, eager as roadkill.

Captain Earl says, "Check out Chef's car."

Chef Ruffhauser slides up the driveway in a BMW with emblems the size of manholes.

A fat man waves to Ruffhauser from the stoop, if you can call it that—it's more a cement porch, or the end stretch of an expressway; the house an obscenity in a water tank, all its features magnified. Three armies could live in there and never find one another.

Fat man is *the* processed-meat magnate—his baloney has a first name and it's his. He's the F. Scott of Wisconsin. Behind his back all The Help call him Fatsby.

Fatsby comes down from his house, walking like an egg in a maroon suit. When he nears, we hear him grunt in the valleys and blow air on the rises of his man-made hills.

Standing next to me, his red head sweats like a sausage. Somehow he kept the suit dry; probably had his pores burnt shut or some other rich-person surgery.

"What in the Helen of Troy is going on *here*?" Fatsby says, smiling, with the weight on *here* since he already knows what goes on everywhere else. He drinks gin in a snifter wide as a church bell.

I stand up.

"Stand up," he says.

"I am standing," I say.

"Well stay that way."

He's beaming, fat and hobbit happy; button-on pork chops for cheeks. Reminds me of this other white guy I saw in a Chinese takeout—ordered the white-meat chicken fried rice; circled it on the sheet menu he handed to the lady. *Ain't no dark meat in there, right?* he said. *'Cause I can't stand dark meat.* He smiled at me. When his order was ready, he asked if they had anything besides Coke.

She said, *We have iced tea.*

Is that root beer? he said.

On his carton a three-tailed bird and a dragon, dancing together or fighting, depending on your mood.

Fatsby says, "We don't sit down. And we don't face the house."

"Don't and don't," I say. "Got it."

He holds out a black ski mask at arm's length. "Here ya go," he says.

"I'm okay. It's not that cold."

Liquor pours from his skin with the smell of fermented pine sap. The ski mask swings in the dusk like a bloody raccoon.

"Really," I say. "It's only September."

He's joyous, insistent. He says, "My daughter works for me. The youngest one. Just so she'll know what it's like. So anyway, she tells me she hears this couple the other day, yeah, *here*"—thumb at the lawn—"at the Ponderson picnic, asking each other when I started hiring Orientals."

I laugh with him. I've become part of his script, about to say something like *You don't gotta tell me twice,* or *You and me both, pal,* but I guess that line's been scratched because he keeps talking.

"I said to her, 'Sure! Bring 'em from Nam, all I care, *for the lawn!*'" He palms my helmet for emphasis, says serious, "You seen them bonsai trees?"

"A picture maybe."

"Well there you go," he says. "So my daughter Carrie. She says, 'Not about the lawn, about the picnic.' I say, 'The picnic?' I mean, between you and me? Front yard, that's where your tour of duty *ends,* my friend. In my backyard? I'll hire a faggot first, just to show you how I feel about Orientals. That's what I tell her. Except the part about the faggots. She's young, she's got friends—you know, she's been to New York a bunch. Her mother loves the place; ask me, it's an outhouse. So I ask around about any Orientals seen at the Ponderson picnic. Come to find out, everyone worked that night's black as stallions," he says. "Except one."

"I guess that's me," I say.

Now he points at me instead of the lawn. "You should try out for one of them game shows," he tells me. "I'm serious." Ice like fingernails float in his snifter. When he drinks you can hear them.

"But I'm not Asian," I say.

"Hell, son, we can both see that," he says. "But. No offense?"

He waits for me to nod.

"Well, no offense, but you're yella as a sick Chink," he says. "And I'll be honest, people don't need reminders of someplace they didn't want to be. Or worse than that, some mistake from a long time ago. When they were drunk or stupid or whatever." He looks between our feet like what he said writhes alive in the grass. Then he says, "Which one of your parents was white?"

Everyone—red, white, black, and blue—asks me this question. Never enough to say somebody died, the next question's always, *How?* And whatever the answer to either one, people look down, watch their shadows trail away from a curb, nodding, *So that's how it happened.*

I say, "My—"

"Guess it doesn't matter," he says. "Can't change the facts afterward."

I tell him my dad used to work for him, that's how I got the job.

"Jiminy Christmas, no shit," he says. "You're Nimrod's kid? Well, we know *he* wasn't the white one!"

Two Thanksgivings ago Fatsby had horse coaches pick up party clients from whatever dead cornfield served for that year's airstrip. It was something's anniversary: ribbons up the coach sides, spoke lights, harness bells; he got the Budweiser Clydesdales.

Dad's assignment sat with wing ice at O'Hare and got sprayed from cranes. Dad waited at the estate in top hat and red tails, nipping whiskey in his done-up fox-hunt taxi and figuring, working for Bud, the horse wants a drink too. So he stole six Guinness from the kitchen to soak the feed bag. They made the whole drop-off—cornfield to mansion—no problem. Only afterward did he race the two of them drunk into a tree.

The Fatsbys gave us a stainless steel vacuum cleaner, wet/dry silverware, a year's worth of cold-cut condolence. Whole thing like a theme present.

Plus the sum of money Mom and I split. When I remember how much, I think I made up the number. I was young and drunk, might as well have stuffed bills in empty bottles and thrown them off a bridge.

Mom took her half to move wherever the Canyon is and pray she doesn't fall in. Now she prays for everything. Now she helps build stilts on her church for the next epic flood.

Hey Ma, you live in the desert.

Great waters come when they will, she says. *We've seen it.* She dances at church with her eyes closed, gaining weight like it makes her more faithful.

Turns out they weren't from Bud and weren't even Clydesdales, just fat horses with dye jobs and false fur boots. Plus it'd been an old horse, always bit the trainer. The stable guy'd said, *I'm glad it's dead.*

*   *   *

"Eyes like loose marbles," Fatsby says, is how my father would gawk at The Help. He's got a whole jukebox of homemade clichés. He says, "I told him, 'Trouble awaits those.' But still, 'You can't oil a wood chair to keep it from squeaking.' I guess that's how you came about. All that squeaking bound to lead to something." He laughs and shakes the ski mask. "So like I said, here ya go." When I don't grab it, he says, "Lighten up, kid, I'm only serious."

I take the mask.

He grins like he just bought lingerie for his daughter. "Put it on," he says.

"I will." I try changing the subject, point my chin at his house. "You got a nice place here. The lawn. Everything. Haven't seen inside, of course."

"Well you don't put cashmere rugs in a tree house, I promise you."

He tips the snifter, swallows what's left, looks in its bottom for more.

"You know they call this stuff divorce juice?" he says. "I drank a tanker already and no luck so far."

We stand there watching the quiet between our faces. I think about nodding.

"So anyway, kid, put on the mask."

"How about when it gets a little colder later?"

"How about now?" he says. "That's it. Now tuck it in the throat there. There ya go. Perfect. Cute as a terrorist. Not like anybody's looking twice anyway, right?"

Up the gravel comes a silver CLK driven by a thick stick of butter with a mustache. His vanity plates say COACH. When past us, he spits in the grass from his Benz window.

Fatsby raises a hand in heil, looks over his shoulders for friends.

"Look at this," Fatsby says. "My party starts, and I'm out in the field talking to the help."

He follows taillights up the driveway.

After Coach, all the guests arrive at once, cars almost hitched at the fenders. The modern-day twenties roar along the lawn behind me.

Across the gravel and way back in the black between crab trees, deer eyes blink like ship lanterns. The undergrowth rearranges its dead wet bed. The bark scratches with hanging animals, eating the trees alive.

The mask easy on the skin as Brillo. My head melts into my shirt. All I can see are the rims of the eyeholes, the trees across the road with squirrels nibbling their fists and squeaking invective.

Captain Earl says, "I'm out of batteries."

I turn my head like my neck's broken. He's checking his hip. For the next five minutes he twitches. He folds his fingers. He whistles. Shifts his weight like a gull on a fence.

Then he says, "Take off that ski mask, man. I keep thinking I'm supposed to kill you."

I can feel my helmet again, can see whatever I want. The mask in the grass, steaming like a hide.

"Stay cool, Yellow," he says. "He already forgot y'all even talked. But pick it up so he don't find it in the morning. Your name's Cole, right?"

"Right."

"Cool. Smoke grass?" he asks, but he's already lit it. "Don't worry." He taps his head. "I got four more in my helmet."

Soon he's so gone he forgets to be a tough guy. Drops his shoulders a little. Smiles in the silence and laughs on his forearms. Other than when I smoked with the Mormon hippie on his Michigan porch surrounded by red wine in coffee cups—all of which, when he found them, were the same mug to him—this is the strangest joint.

Dark completes itself. The oak herd swallows its shadows, holding them black in the trunks. The electric light gains confidence, brighter in the branches and lying in pieces on the lawn.

Captain Earl says, "I used to dishwash." Tells me his stepbrother Vince still does. Holds up his hand and spreads his fingers. "Neither one of us got no fingerprints."

"You saw that in a movie."

"May be," he says. "But I still ain't got fingerprints." He tells me no more cars are coming. His brother had counted the number of set plates, and Captain Earl counted heads at the gate. "And if you call me Captain one more time . . ." he says.

But he seems all right, more real than the cartoon niggers who worked the picnic, even if he is short and complex-vexed, hand in his shirt warming a gun or a holstered fetus. Lantern somewhere around his knees.

He looks over his shoulder, says, "Here come Carrie."

I turn, expecting a blood-soaked prom dress. Instead, her hips carve shape in her silhouette. She slings them side to side like she seeds fields for a living. She knows people pay attention when she walks.

She stands before us, marcelled blond in waitstaff black and white, bending every right place in her silk black pants, balancing an empty tray weighed down with darkness.

I close my mouth. "Say, Shirley Temple."

"Shirley Temple," she says. "Haven't heard that one in the last five minutes."

She's got eyes the sockets run away from, and I remember her from the first day—burning holes in my head behind her living room glass, watching me walk to the furnace.

"I saw you at the picnic," I say.

"Oh? You were here?"

"But with different hair."

"You had the same stupid helmet on, I wouldn't be able to tell," she says. She stares at the back of my brain, smiles now, bloody lipstick in the corners of her teeth like meat off the bone. "So, you boys want drinks?"

Earl says, "You know what I want."

She says, "Yeah, I *know*. But I forgot."

He orders Courvoisier and cranberry. I order Jack and whatever.

"Whatever what?" she says.

"Whatever you got."

"No," she says. "You're supposed to say please. Didn't your mother teach you how to act?"

"My dad taught me everything. Mostly late night, when he was drunk." I smile like I'm running out of teeth.

"And that's got *what* to do with me?" she says.

She sends laughs through the still-shaking trees as she leaves us.

Suddenly the night's ecstatic on its edges. Electricity traces the leaves—as if I forgot today's my birthday or swallowed a sparkler.

"She's incredible," I say.

"She's so full of shit her name stinks," says Earl. He passes me a fresh-lit. "I seen this episode already. If you knew her you'd see right through this shit. Instead, you gonna walk around here dragging your tongue, and this lawn'll be cleaner when she get up in the morning." He takes a hit, squints, pulls his chin back like I hit him in the throat, and stretches out. "That's what's gonna happen. Dig out your heart with a plastic spoon."

I told him there were times I'd stare at what girls picked for art—a poster of kittens chewing on the same old pink yarn ball, subtitled *Ain't friendship great!* Or the Seurat with the park and the rich people watching a river. Getting dorm-room head beneath the laminated replica, I'd think, *Would anyone dressed that nice ever step in the grass?* But Carrie would, and she did, and all to come see me.

Earl says, "I think you better let me hold on to this, 'cause I don't know what the fuck you talking about anymore. She always come down and bring us drinks."

"Yeah, but this time she came down different."

"You never even seen her before."

"She's got the black pants," I say.

"They all got black pants."

"No, like the *black* pants. Like hot pants. But black."

"Jesus," Earl says. "And I did this to him."

Our lanterns lay sideways in the grass, blacking their glass. Gravel climbs into a paintable landscape, the crab fruit glowing something holy.

Earl sears his lips and fingers on what's still burning, the orange lying in every line of his face.

"She's the kind of girl—you send her your ear in the mail, right? The one without the earring, and she be like, 'What. You couldn't send me the good one?'" He flicks a spark that blows away before it lands. "That's what they're like," he says. "Always seem like a good idea at the time."

In the house, the party crosses all windows.

Earl says, "Blow out your fire and let's go see about them drinks."

We step down into the lawn with our dead lanterns behind us, the little hills wet with night. We kick up spray smells of piss and ginger ale, sparking when it catches light, damping pants in the dark of the valleys. A lawn long as allegory—like at the end we're supposed to realize something, realize everything we just came from and what it meant, look back at our passage and appreciate where we stand now.

But we're not there yet. Still kicking the light out of the grass, still dodging oaks and hiding behind their blackness from snipers lying on the roof.

Earl says, "The light ain't gonna shoot you."

"If they see us, though."

"You keep staying in the same place, you got your own problems. I'm not waitin."

He walks away from my crouch, half of him lit, half in shadow.

We make it to the side of the house, to the locker-room front door coned under a lamp bright as a pig-size firefly.

The locker room's a converted stable with a handwritten sign above the horse door that says HELP in charcoal letters, edges flaking off as you read them. I've been inside twice. Between it and the house is a skinny addition The Help call the decompression chamber—tuxes and French-maid jump skirts on a rack under heat lamps, like they're lamb ribs, or perishable, like anything expensive.

The stable itself is just a wide room and no lockers, splintered pegs set in the wall, head hanging as if they've been climbed on. Whoever converted it left the horse partitions, left the hay, added green-yellow hairy new wood benches that hurt to sit on.

When we walk past, Earl spits on the door.

Almost at the kitchen now. Where the woods start is a doorless toolshed with two rottweilers strapped to it. The right one's got a head you'd have to own a T-top to

take in the car, calm and staring—the worst kind—when
they snap they never miss, and you don't get bit, you lose
a limb. The left dog sniffs weed clumps, tests the end of
his leather leash. He hops around, thinks about standing,
waves his unsheathed pink and wanders toward the dark
behind the shed. A hose in the lawn, splayed like lost
intestines.

Carrie and a black guy share Chinese from a carton
on the kitchen back steps. She's got noodles strung from
her teeth to her chopsticks. The brother's eyes the color of
dead custard.

"That's Vince," Earl whispers. "Keep a hand on
your wallet."

"Thought he was your brother."

"Stepbrother," Earl says. "I mean, he's a brother.
Just not mine."

Vince the dishwasher's got circular scars sliding
across his face like someone got him with an apple corer
or a car lighter. He shakes my hand, looking away like he's
taking a bribe. Skin like a burlap sack.

Carrie smiles with a greasy mouth, says, "Oh my
God, I forgot your drinks." She and Vince pass their own
joint. "I'd offer," she says. "But he gave it to me."

She points at Vince and disappears to the kitchen
with a hit in her throat.

Vince smokes, points at Earl.

Earl points at me, says, "I guess I only had three in
my helmet."

Vince says, "Want some? It's cold."

He holds out the carton: a clotted puddle of brown-green noodles and nearly colorless vegetables. He pulls it away before anyone answers.

She comes back with two drinks gold as apple juice, hands them off like grenades with the pins pulled, their tops spilling in the dirt.

Earl holds his up to the light. "Where's the cranberry?"

"In the kitchen," she says.

Vince makes a thick wet noise with the lo mein. Bugs knock a conga on the lamp. The trees throw wind around in their dresses. Between us, smoke the only thing speaking.

The quick things happen like this: You stand there, wondering could you fit inside a Chinese carton with the sides greased enough, watching the weeds celebrate at the front of a dust-smothered shed. The waitress grabs your hand and squints up at you as if it means something. The brothers start up; spit on each other during words, clash teeth, rip their own lips off, furious about pro city teams you're almost sure you've heard of.

They've chosen sides, and in among the vague you worry you'll root wrong. You look at her. She still squints, you might even call it a smile, her eyes on a train track or a dust storm coming, or wind, or distance—all of it, and her warmth along your arm with the confidence of weather, and she smiles like the right direction.

Carrie drags me willing into the woods, back where it's blackest. Or not that dark but at least where the house light runs out of breath and lays fingers on the last leaf it can touch. The deer find a darkness even farther, still signaling with their pairs of lamps. They stand stock solid with the weight of nothing to do, like watching from an attic crack while people rob your house.

Carrie kicks leaves away in a narrow square, long as a grave.

"Don't you hate my father?" she says. "The way he treats you? The ski mask? I mean, don't you hate that?"

"I know I don't like the way he looks at me."

"No. Do you *hate* it?"

"Like he runs a zoo and fucks all the animals."

She says, "I'd hate it."

I sit on a tree stump wide enough to cork a reactor.

"I guess you could say I *do,* in fact, hate him."

"I mean, what do you get out of dressing like a horse-riding midget?" she says.

"I didn't dress like this. They made me."

Everything runs beneath me like the next square of film, my heels catching in the roots of the escalator. I watch Carrie's face turn, into what or where I can't tell.

"And what's he pay you?" she says. " A hackeysack an hour? Please."

She says it *po-lice,* slow and split in half.

Eventually I use the word "hate" in enough sentences to convince her. She relaxes. She sits on the stump in poses she must practice at home. Like she wants me to take notes, or sculpt her, tell her to love the camera. She lurches forward, and in kisses our teeth spark like claws.

"I don't even know you," she moans, sucking breath off my face.

"People who don't know each other can say everything."

She looks back at me, around me. I didn't know my head had that many sides. When I find her eyes, they won't both work without the brights on—one's dim, the other's glare makes my brain hurt.

I squint. She thinks I'm smiling and kisses me worse than ever. Spit boils. We shuck each other's clothes like husks.

She lies naked across the rings of the tree stump. She writhes in subtle laughter, soft as spores and bending in places I never knew possible. The sweat on the small of her back parading against my fingers. The braille of her cold skin. She smells like crayon food, like hollandaise candles.

The deer leave. Trees inch away, pull up roots, ashamed and scattering, plugging vomit with branches. In the noise of us, in the smell of what we create, the mud around us fills with water from underneath, where trees used to be.

I've got the heat of her in my crotch, the skin on skin of now, our tongues mixing like viscera, when someone screams, "Carrie!" and at first I think it's me.

We stop with me inside her. From here and between the trees, we see Fatsby call her from the steps behind the kitchen. He screams other names. Names like Vince! Or Earl! Names I'm almost sure I've heard before.

The quick things happen again—except now I'm

cold and wet in the wrong places, and naked, and she whispers *shit* and *shit* and *shit* again, breathing like I punched out her wind.

She grows back her outfit in a time-lapse moss of shame, says, "I *knew* I shouldn't have followed you out here. Now I'm dead."

She's already sprinting for the house before my heels finish sinking in the mud.

"Dad! Dad! Dad!" plays off the trees.

The moon took the night off. The trees are back again, close as older sisters, exhaling and furious—mean enough to make me put my clothes on, to feel the need for explanation. The spaces between their trunks hum. My jockey sleeve's mucked to the shoulder.

When I get back behind the kitchen there's nobody but the rotts by the toolshed, yanking the end of their tethers and panting me questions.

Vince comes from the woods with a whiskey fifth finished to the bar code. He takes two steps back to go forward, and soon he's so close he hits me in the chest with the bottle.

"Want some?" he says. "It's warm."

"Where'd everybody go?"

"What's up with your shirt?" he says. "You know you gotta pay for that. Like I give a *shit!*" he screams in a whisper. He laughs, wags the whiskey neck before the dogs. "Here kitty, kitty, kitty."

"Where's Carrie?"

"Inside somewhere." He drinks the liquor, shakes with its seizure.

"Earl?"

"He went for the lawn when the trouble started." Vince coughs on his knees, spit in strings off his lips.

"This is bad." I run to the back of the house, to the nearest window, all lights out in this living room and emptiness in the one hallway I can see.

Vince stinks over my shoulder.

He says, "This wouldn't be half this good if y'all hadn't been fuckin." He smiles, claps without sound, answers my look with, "Hey man, I was back there too. Where's I supposed to go?"

I look around the yard for exits. There's one small piece of food left from the picnic—a broken bun with its pinched-off end of bratwurst.

"She'll tell him," I say. "He'll kill me."

Vince stares at the roof, squinting at the sheer fact of gutters.

"Then we kill him first," he says. He knocks me away from the window. "Hang him with his own hose. Out front. Where everyone'll find him in the morning."

Things start to make sense. My options double.

"You could do it, Vince. You got no fingerprints."

"Shit, they gonna know who it was, that's not the point." He stands straight as a marine, flinging orders. "Hold this," he says. He hands me the whiskey. "Follow me. Give the dogs some of that."

He runs away in a crouch.

★   ★   ★

I forget to follow. I drink. I go to a different window, to a few, finally to the one with people in it—Fatsby and his fat wife pressing their heads together until they're lopsided, dancing like a dump truck in a three-point turn. The ten others rich enough to stay late take up all the small couches. I wait for Carrie to come burning through the door. I wonder what keeps her.

The window's cracked a touch and streaming heat. The fireplace is a nightmare. The rug swims around within itself trying to be Oriental. Everyone and their teeth swaying from the gums.

Vince comes back with an iron chair.

He says, "I couldn't find the hose."

"What's that?"

"A chair." Vince sits in it. "Just shut up and let me think."

He picks lint off his shirt.

The room swings big band on vinyl. Smoke shortens the ceiling. Maybe Carrie's never coming.

Vince touches the circles on his face. In this light they're brighter, light blue and shining. He doesn't like the look of things.

"I got an idea," he says.

He's up, chair off the ground in his fists.

I want to tell him wait. Tell him hold on. Tell him maybe.

But decisions are finished. He puts the chair through the window, glass screaming like a bell exploded, shards bouncing off our temples, our throats, our crotches, and into the room where everyone waits for theirs.

What Good Is You Anyway?

MY DAD LOST HIS LEFT LEG, SO HE HAS TO DRIVE AN AUTOMATIC. My mom's remarried and forgotten him. Everything makes him equally angry. You could simply flip through channels when he suddenly screams, "WOULD YOU JUST CHOOSE SOMETHING AND LEAVE IT?" using his crutch to smash every bottle on the coffee table.

We cohabitate, as they say. When he did a year for his sixth drunk driving, Mom divorced him quickly. She moved across town with her long-term boyfriend, to a loft overlooking the fish market. I commandeered the brownstone to help everyone out and couldn't have been happier: year out of college and an entire place to myself, satellite dish, Dad's car and liquor cabinet, Mom to remind me of electric bills and other such necessaries, since everything was in her name. I could smash empty bottles on the walls or throw them through screens in the summer. I could drag the barbeque inside to grill, black up the ceiling with smoke, all so I wouldn't miss a minute of the World Cup Semi. Then they released him and he moved in with me going on six drunken months now.

Other than that we're like most fathers and sons: not much to say, never live up to the other's expectations. We head through life frustrated and furious toward Customer Service, hoping for some kind of refund.

*   *   *

He drives me to the bus I take to work. He slouches, splits traffic in his hatchback Citation. Dashboard so ash-covered you'd think he parked next to a volcano with the windows open. Crutches and golf clubs clack in the back—tangled shafts, iron heads pushing between the front seats to see out the windshield—whole mess like tropical plants in a mulch of yellow newspaper and empty Merit cartons.

They're not really crutches. They're the special kind, metal bands wrap around your forearms. Crutches are temporary. These things say disease; they say permanence. They fit in the golf bag.

I look at him.

He's black, I'm half, but that's his fault 'cause his wife's white. Was white. I mean *ex*-wife. Mom's still white.

He turns away from driving, stares me sincere in the eye, and says, "You sittin on my cigarettes?" He swerves, shatters his blinker light sliding past a cab fender, sticks his head out the window, "YOU FUCKING NIGERIAN!" Honks so hard he rips off the horn cover and throws it in back.

He pulls a smashed pack from beneath his ass, lights a bent cigarette preening toward the ceiling like a trunk. The leg stops just where his knee used to be. Pants folded under and sewn to the back. He lets me out at the bus stop and pulls away honking with the door still open.

*   *   *

Dad refuses a wheelchair and the entire concept of pros-thetics. "Let's just keep things manual long as possible," he'll say. "What's left anyway. Go bring me something."

I think he does it to have weapons on hand at all times and cheap-shot people's Achilles in crowds and crosswalks. In a bar parking lot I saw him bring up the rub-ber stopper in a guy's larynx. He's invented some sort of crutch-wielding one-foot kung fu he practices in front of the basement wall of mirrors, both turntables going, Chi-nese opera and Gil Scott-Heron at equal volume.

One of his crutches has a detachable cup holder. If he looks down and finds it on the left one he'll switch.

He's got a bright orange dent-rusted kickstand he breaks out only for the driving range. A different one if he's playing nine or eighteen that's black metal and shiny as patent leather.

He won't talk about prison except to say his foot-ball connections kept him from getting raped.

"And drafted," I'll say.

"Fuck you," he'll tell me. Sometimes he grabs at cramps in his phantom calf, holding an invisible ball to his stump.

Only a few sad suits at the bus stop this morning, other than mine. Pollen balls fall from the trees. Bleary-eyed white guy next to me, hacking and wheezing like he swallowed a cat. On a bench ten feet away an old black man gums brown sugar from a paper sack. Tiny white beard perched on a pyramid of dirty wool sweaters.

Then there's an accident, right at this intersection.

First the tire screech, then air explodes metal, loud enough to scalp you. One second, average morning traffic, the next a car bent and buried halfway under a truck—delivery doors smashed open, vegetables spraying off the car trunk, rolling for the gutters.

Everyone from blocks around swarms the corner, burning their hands trying to pull apart folded steel. Some return to their cars, reversing to make room for EMS.

After that it's pneumatics and hydraulics. Giant saws. Firemen and paramedics shishing in fluorescent clothes like ghosts. Even with caged lights and sparks in the grease puddles, they can't find an answer.

The truck driver is crying, head between his knees on a bench by the bank of pay phones.

I've forgotten work by this point. I just stand arms folded with everyone else, sweating. Some people brought out lawn chairs. Some carry pets, laughing. Children kick balls around the outskirts of the crowd. A guy sells incense that smells of burnt rubber bands. It's become a street fair, each corner with its clique and grill—Caribbean, Mexican, soul. One corner has drunks sharing pint bottles and cigarettes, all pissing in the same trash can.

A man runs along the curbs herding onions and dumping them in his stroller. His infant thinks it's funny, picks at the skins. The crowd drips trash in the street.

A lady near me tells someone, "Ain't nobody said they legally dead yet. Have a little faith."

Her kid seems disappointed. He says, "Lemme get a seat," scratching at his throat for a seam.

"There ain't none," she says, as she sits on two chairs stacked one atop the other.

A month ago I was on a subway train that derailed. Pulling from the station and *slam*. Threw me across a seat, into a pole, back in the seat I'd come from. All the kids and old people crying, holding their arms or legs or heads. Dirt smoke filled the car. A young dread with blood on her face, slapping the doors with her palm.

The conductor came on: "Ladies and gentlemen, obviously we had an accident. I'm hurt too, but I'ma try and stay up and hold on. Until help gets here." *In which case, I'ma lay down and die,* he didn't say. But later I read in the paper he did exactly that.

A different MTA guy entered the car and screamed, "Everyone remain calm! Doors will open shortly." Million keys on a ring off his belt. He half opened the door closest to me and stepped on the platform.

For three seconds nobody did anything. Then everyone slammed into one another running for the crack to escape. I was already gone by that point, striding the steps a flight at a time.

Once at a baseball game I saw a fat man in my section fall in the aisle as his heart exploded. I imagined a basketball murdered point-blank, with a pillow for a silencer and enough air pressure to bust an eardrum. His fist still crushed its pretzel, mustard in his knuckles. For three innings the bleachers stayed somber. Uniforms attempted resuscitation and electrocution before carting the corpse off under a sheet on a stretcher. Then we hit a lead-off homer in the eighth to go up 4–3 and everyone forgot about it.

And after each of these—whether walking in the sun, buying beer in the bleachers, or sitting on a picnic bench eating peanut butter and jelly—I always find myself smiling, having just seen an accident, at least heard one, and for the first and last time in months truly feel blood in every limb, present and accounted for.

Just before they extract the smashed bodies I leave, decide to cut work entirely. Feel like I should be skipping and whipping a stick against fence slats.

Up the street a cop sits on a sawhorse, blocking off the service road. He's got a makeshift caution-tape fence and his car horizontal just in case.

A woman in a shawl pushes a stroller up to me on the sidewalk. Dark eyebrows for miles. Same with the baby. "Can we go down there?" her fabric asks me.

"There's been an accident."

"I see that. Can I cross though is what I'm asking."

"Yeah, you can cross. If you're walking. You just can't drive."

She looks down into her stroller. "Always something," she says.

Half block past the cop and around the corner comes Nam, an army-green Chevy Nova always moves in slow motion, plays only Hendrix, weed smoke billowing from its windows, driven by two brothers who played college ball with my father thirty-some years ago. Football kept them all from getting drafted.

They stop beside me, windows blasting "Who Knows." Frog rides shotgun, a still-skinny wideout, eyes where his temples should be and an immaculately spherical Afro. Luther drives, dark-skinned ex–defensive lineman, fills up that entire side of his vehicle. Luther had a short stint with the Redskins before compound fractures in both fibulae on the same play. He's gargantuan, three-inch calluses on each forearm from a youth spent smacking cinder-block pillars in his Mississippi basement.

"What it is," Frog says. "Why you ain't at work? What's with the cop? Frienda yours?"

I thumb down street. "Accident," I say. "Car went under a truck."

They start hopping up and down like they just stole their parents' car. "Yo, yo, get in," Frog says, tilts his seat forward, presses his face against the glove compartment.

I climb in back onto smashed CD cases and a dirty nervous collie.

"Say hi Ella," Frog tells the dog. "She don't bite. She can sing though. Sing Ella! Sing!"

Ella howls in my ear, jabs paws at my ribs and throat. Two months ago someone dog-sat Ella and she jumped from the convertible doing sixty-five on the highway, ripped her paws off. What grew back feels like asphalt.

Frog sings with her, "Stormy weather . . ."

"That ain't Ella," says Luther.

"Who then, Mr. Jazzolympics? You don't know."

"Ain't Ella."

"Just drive down to the accident, man. Let's see some shit."

"You can't go down there," I say. "Hence the cop."

Frog and Luther visibly deflate, turn their faces on me. Frog says, "What good is you anyway?"

These two, my dad, and ten others founded Groove Phi Groove: a black frat at Morgan State that now has a national charter and still calls Dad for donations. They send us multiple black mugs with the G Phi G insignia, crowned with the thirteen founding-father stars.

"Which star are you?" I'll ask Dad.

"The one who's done enough and don't owe those niggers no money," he'll say.

One Orange Bowl morning during warm-ups for their one and only black college bowl game, Luther shivered my father's helmet in half. Dad lay bleeding with his head exposed, except for the section of helmet between his head and the grass.

"Jesus mother fuck," said Dad.

"I guess so, Dave. I'm sorry," Luther said.

Dad played the whole game with a head bandage. For years afterward Frog'd tell this story and say, "You know, like that flute guy in the Independence Day band. Might've been the drummer. Can't remember."

Then Luther'll say, "I did you a favor, Dave. You ain't never looked that good."

Supposedly Luther and Frog once argued whether the Maxwell House theme was music or percolation.

Frog said, "Ain't a coffee pot in the *world,* ever sang a song while it got ready."

"It's the pot, man," Luther said.

"That ain't a goddamn pot."

"It's the pot."

"It's music!" Frog said. "One of them—you know what I mean—jingle thingamajigs!"

Luther got up and threw the TV through the dorm lounge window. "I said it's the motherfucking pot," he said. "You see. Niggers don't listen."

Nowadays, you can usually find Frog down at the Civic Center, outside the weight-loss convention with a bag of candy bars and two different shoes on. He's still quick, though, he'll tell you, catch a fly between his knuckle and the bar brick. See things that ain't really coming. He calls it a talent.

These are my father's only friends. I find him in their mouths and gestures.

They smoke grass and don't offer. Ella the collie's comatose, head out the window and gazing at the gas tank. We're out on the expressway, Luther laughing.

"Look at this motherfucker," Frog says about me.

"*This* motherfucker," Luther says.

"Never," says Frog. "At *no time,* do you get ass. Ever. Yet and still you gone have the nerve to work at Mattress Discounter."

"Have the nerve," Luther says.

"And in a suit," Frog says. "Every morning up at the bus stop like you somebody. Like you know somethin bout a mattress. Meanwhile, you sleepin in a hammock in your mama's old shoe box."

"*Shoe* box. She don't even have two."

"She gotta cram both feet in the same damn shoe and hop to work."

"Where we going?" I ask.

"See Luther? All these young brothers, not a one'll fess up."

Luther sucks his teeth, shakes his head, "It's a shame is what it is."

Frog says, "*Damn* shame."

My dad lost the leg walking drunk through an intersection. He tells people he was headed for his rental car with every intention of driving, so it could've been worse. He'll say his real car was in the driveway with a few DWIs on it, like parking tickets he forgot to pull off. Then he says, "Make that several DWIs," and laughs, sort of.

Meanwhile his real car had tubes in its doors you had to blow into, below the legal limit else they wouldn't unlock or even open at all. That was too much, in his terms. For his last arrest he rented a blue Cavalier and weaved around town. Hit a public bus as it took on passengers.

Back at the station the cops had questions:

Why were you driving a rental car?

"Car was in the shop."

What about the weaving and slurring of words?

"Slight stroke a few years ago, haven't been the same since."

Smell of liquor on your breath?

"I had a wine sauce with dinner."

The fact you'd defecated yourself?

"Can't say I remember that."

I ask again, "Where, exactly, are we headed?"

"Hey, Luther. Half-man in back wants to know where we're headed."

Luther says, "Ain't none of your goddamn—what was the question?"

Ella's turned toward us, panting to see what'll happen as we laugh past oncoming traffic.

Ends up we're headed for the landfill.

When we get there it's a half-empty parking lot walled off with high cement platforms and long narrow pit compactors full of cracked bags. This isn't the actual *landfill,* of course, just the lobby where they prepare waste before it's set among the trash hills.

We pull everything from the trunk across the gravel, Ella skipping and yipping among us, licking up garbage juice. We drag bags of laundry and vegetables, curdled magazines, fast-food trash, black frat coffee mugs, broken ashtrays, and bent sand wedges.

For the eight hundred and seventy-ninth time, Luther tells us about when he broke in their super's apartment through the fire escape to piss on the couch. How he had to remove the plastic first, and when he finished took it with him. Same plastic that's on his couch right now.

The landfill crawls with flying squirrels, only here we call them pigeons. Jaded, urban squirrels, growing lewd in spite of themselves. We've also got trash gulls, covered in some kind of feather fungus.

The three of us light our own smokes and throw the last bags over the edge. We're lucky enough to be here when the compactor smashes everything in its teeth to a cube. Luther kicks Ella back down the steps so she doesn't get mangled. Soon the dump trucks will come to feed.

"Welp," Frog says, "there go that."

"Thank God," says Luther.

Gray-black clouds fill the sky, undersides dirty where they scrape along the earth. Crushed ghosts and smoke, demons in the corners of the parking lot. Ella's limping between pickups, barely letting her left front paw touch ground, like she stepped on a nail. Frog almost falls down the steps.

Through those trees is the decrepit deli. Past that a YWCA leaned over at the fourth floor and peering in the street. A few blocks farther sits my house, gleaming and upright as a gold tooth in the afternoon.

"You know what guys," I say. "I'ma walk home."

Leaned on a car trunk, wincing and rubbing his shin, Frog says, "Well I'm sorry our chariot ain't good enough, mister Bed Technician."

"You know that ain't it," I say.

"What is it then?" Frog asks.

Luther staring at his thumb. Dump trucks roll through the gate with a low growl, arrogant as tanks. Anything I say'll be strangled in noise.

One time Dad was pulled over speeding on 95 South. Sergeant came to the window, showed him red numbers on the back of his speed gun.

"Know how fast you were goin?" Sarge asked.

Dad said, "Where do I blow into it?"

Worst part is Sarge laughed and let him go with a no seat belt ticket.

Now Dad drives sober, with vengeance and a suspended license, urgent to lose his other leg. When he drinks he stays in the backyard, far from the car as possible, back to the fence, and he faces the house. Even in winter.

I left Frog and Luther with a wave and between the trees the leaves were still wet, even with no rain in days. I made it home, snuck in the front door, took a nap in my suit.

At six-thirty I head downstairs, find Dad out back, drunk and tangled in the hammock. Crutches in the grass, sports talk on radio.

When I get close he says, "Now, what I want to know is, how you gonna go and lose by twenty-eight? To the team dead last in your division."

"Me?" I say.

"At home no less."

"Here?"

"You know what your problem is?" Dad says. "You don't listen."

He shakes his cigarette pack in the air. The last of his smokes and some loose tobacco fall on his face.

"You shouldn't smoke," I say.

"I don't have a leg," he smiles.

He's wearing shorts. He knows no one needs to see this. His one shin's knotted with bent bone and calcium deposits, the muscle lumped and cratered, barbeque skin, whole thing like it's been through a wood chipper and plastered back together. I remember an ambulance man describing him laid out in the intersection: "His legs was so mangled it looked like a squid." Now Dad's got a Pinocchio hinge for an ankle, but he can set it on the ground and that's all he cares about.

He tells me Frog's woman Cattie just called. She said Frog and Luther had them an accident over by the landfill. "And what the hell happened to your suit?" Dad says. "You sleepin at work again? No wonder you can't sell nothin."

That's true. In the last four months I've sold a trundle, a twin, and a cot. Manager called me into his office. "Your recent sales have been incredible," he said. "Ridiculous really, if you stop to think about it half a sec."

I thought maybe he'd pulled the wrong file, or I'd just been hard on myself. Either way I was looking at a raise. Then the manager said, "And I don't mean the good kind."

I tell Dad, "I slept on the bus."

"On the floor?"

"What about Frog and Luther?" I say.

"They're in the hospital."

"Shouldn't we go over there?"

"Those motherfuckers didn't come to *my* hospital," he says. "Or jail. Besides, they be all right. They got insurance. All those machines. They're fine. Dog's dead though."

"Ella?"

"I guess. Went through the windshield."

"What else'd Cattie say?"

"She never liked that dog anyhow," he says.

Turns out Luther and Frog rear-ended a pickup. For all we know they're laid out in a building downtown and still have most of their own blood.

Dad chews on his tongue. Advice is coming. His usually takes the form of things like, "Never trust the guy in the locker room takes his pants off before his shirt."

Before I went to Amsterdam he told me, "Don't kill anybody. And don't bring anything back."

"I'm not stupid."

"But you do stupid things," he'd said. Every now and then he had a point.

I expect now he'll say, *You can't drive fucked up. Trust me.*

Instead he says, "Poor bastards." He rubs his chin with his wrist. "Just don't do what I did."

"What's that?"

"Hell," he says. "I can't remember."

*   *   *

At his worst he used to hide miniature liquor under leaves in this same yard—stuff he bought by the case or swiped off flights for the ease with which they slipped into sleeves, hats, car-seat covers; he'd memorize the pattern on the back of a leaf, its position in relation to the fence. Tell Mom he was taking a walk out back. Always found interesting things in the grass. Things he'd hold to his face and get a closer look at.

Now, right out in the open, he's got a handle of Jack set on a stool and a stainless bucket of ice. Somehow this is better than before. The simple fact it's visible. An admission almost. A step in the right direction.

"A hangover of a thousand miles begins with," he said when he first moved back in and pulled out the fifth of whiskey. He answered my look with, "I'll make it last."

Which he did. For exactly two days.

"May be a little watered down by now," he says as he hands me my drink he's made already. He clinks his glass against mine in cheers, which might seem a little thing, but you don't know the man.

He says, "It'll be the size of a bathtub, but I still want a pool out here." He's said that for years.

I lean against the fence and we watch the house.

"But first we need to get one of them machines," he says, waves a hand over the backyard. "Move the earth."

Polly Here
Somewhere

I MARRY MY IMAGINARY FRIEND WHEN I'M SEVEN, IN A CERE-mony beneath the seesaw. Her name's Polly and she looks like whatever I think of—sometimes the Morton Salt girl skipping in the rain, almost kicking up her slicker just enough to see her underwear, sometimes Coppertoned and half naked and her puppy's got her panties in its teeth.

On the playground it's raining. Rubber swings hang on chains; there's a box full of drop-pocked sand. The seesaw's no shelter because the weather's too sideways. For our wedding she's the Salt Girl who forgot her umbrella and needs me to wipe water from her eyes.

I have two green candy rings with lime-flavored diamonds but when I slip hers on it falls off.

A stray dog walks up, puts a urine puddle in the mulch where her candy sits. We squat and watch the steam.

When I eat my ring, I chew with my mouth open so at least she can see it.

My white mom and black dad hunch in gray slumps at opposite sides of the house, watching snow fall in fistfuls. Somewhere along the ground floor I push on a wall, wondering aloud where the stairs went.

At night from their room come dull thuds and grunts, like they're rolling downhill in a coffin. My pajamas have feet

and I'm stuck to the door at the ear. Polly's invisible, hiding in the dark. She shivers when she can't understand
something.

Then the bed creaks, robe snaps like a flag, Mom
blows through the door, smiling with force enough to throw
me into the bathroom. I get a gash in the back of my head
from a cabinet handle, a two-inch scar where my Afro won't
grow in the future.

She's still sweating from bed but no longer smiling.

She says, "Oh baby, I didn't even know you were
there!"

I try adultery at ten, because you can't touch what you
imagine.

Hope and I sit on a piss-proof lime vinyl mattress
in the unmade room, wet bathing suits inside out beneath
our feet. Our mothers share the cottage, sit downstairs
watching the one o'clock soap. Polly conveniently down at
the beach.

Hope flips a coin to see who does what. I lose.

She's got sand in the lines where her suit pinched.
On the nightstand a six-inch whittled sailor with a stiff
wooden leg. Gulls grow on wires from dock stumps around
his foot.

Hope doesn't really taste like anything.

That night I still feel her thighs on my face, but even
having touched someone inside I'll never be closer to anyone than Polly. Lying next to her in the black, she speaks on

my throat: "Every time you breathe, I can smell something wrong with you. Wherever you are I'm in your head."

It's '82. She tells me all the world will explode for what I did. My parents go first, and all the bombs of Russia are pointed at my crotch.

At twelve I sit in a strip club's tip row next to a tiny mongoose of a white kid whose name I don't know. He's my age but hairy, one long eyebrow. Then there's Billy Joker, with his fish head and glasses. He's white too, blue sweater, lemon buttons, and his dad runs the place.

It's called Creamy Gene's. He's got the strobe light going, the requisite disco ball, the lit-up cylinders of polka dots that blink and spin and flash on asses.

Fifteen minutes to the noon lunch rush, just setting up the buffet. On a stool at the back of the stage sits the afternoon's first act, forty years old in a red sequin bikini, running a finger along her cesarean scar.

Polly's behind me. I feel her arms cross and, when her head shakes, her hair on my neck.

In the center of the circle stage, fully clothed Billy twirls around the brass pole. He's got all the acts memorized. From the DJ booth his dad screams names and Billy does impressions.

"Gina!" screams Gene.

Now Billy walks like a cowgirl, hands on invisible guns. He shoots air and blows on his fingertips. He sings eyes-closed with the disco, slips his hands along his hips.

"Job opening!" his dad says in the mic.

Billy does the splits, he smiles, he somersaults his back to a pole, and grips his zipper.

"All right, that's enough," Gene says. "Save it for the customers."

Billy climbs down and me and Mongoose clap and hoot, splash our flat Cokes.

"Rapture" comes on and in his pro PA voice Gene screams at red bikini, "Only ten minutes till we open Eiiileeeeen! How bout working up a sweat and givin the kids a freebie!"

"Those piss ants wouldn't know a good piece if it shit in their hair!" she says loud over Blondie. "*You* dance for 'em!"

Gene shuts up, lets the song go, tests the red and blue sirens.

And then, among the lights and the empty circle of everything, Polly takes the stage, one hand on her waist, one up under her hair, swinging her set of hula-hoop hips. She dances better than Billy but doesn't love it so much. She'd squat and bounce on her heels without your attention. She doesn't need an audience to watch herself in the sectioned mirror.

Of course, it's only me who sees her anyway. Everyone else watches Eileen throat something from behind her sinuses and spit it on everyone's reflection.

In the dark gym of an eighth-grade talent contest/break-off a speckled kid with puberty all over his face backspins in a painted lane. The crowd of teens steams, standing so close to one another. The nets drip. The speakers scream, "Rock, Rock, Planet Rock!" Billy, Mongoose, and the rest of my friends grope through shirts for tiny bras. They all have girls to spill Coke on, girls with braces that grate your lips and teeth but at least you feel something.

"It's not that I don't want to," Polly says. "I just *can't.*"

"That's worse," I say.

We hang out in the locker-room doorway, away from the crowd, for reasons like I got Hendrix hair but can't play guitar. Or break-dance.

"I'm supposed to grow out of you by now," I tell Polly.

She sits on the bench where boys change. She says, "You're still just a little kid. Grabbing at anything it can reach."

We stand in silence, watch colored lights slide across the court.

"If you were human, or I was imaginary, maybe it'd work out," I say.

"And if I were real," she says. "You wouldn't even believe I was me."

Freshman year in high school and who knew all I needed was a haircut. Now my scar shows but the girls like to pet it. I start getting looks like in cartoons when the paint can falls on the invisible man.

I try to stop thinking about Polly but she's everywhere—on the toilet while I shower, holding up poles in
the school bus aisle, sitting and smiling on a Home Ec oven
when in the middle of muffins April Scott asks, "How many
erections do you get a day?"

Polly says this whole sex thing's a phase—"And
you'll come back when it passes." She whispers it on April's
back, where the field hockey number 1 shows through her
apron straps. April's smiling at me, clicking the pair of tongs
in her hand.

Today changes the rest of my life. April waits until
Psychology, and instead of wet swim suits and "You wanna
play light in the socket?" she turns in her seat and says, "We
should have sex today."

So I say, "Okay."

She's a year older. We leave at lunch and she lets
me drive without my license.

In the rearview Polly recedes, crying on the curb.
For the first time since the beach she isn't with me, and I
feel like I just pissed on my sister.

And later I feel something else, April using Vaseline
lip therapy for lubrication and it takes a while to squeeze
enough out of the tube.

For the rest of high school I feel like Paul Bunyan. I get a
girlfriend named Mary who kisses like a mule biting a car-
rot. But she drives her mom's Mercedes and also plays field
hockey in plaid skirts and knee socks. I hardly notice Polly's
still around, me and Mary have so much sex—in backyards,
showers, and sand traps, on her porch at four in the morn-

ing with the paper thrown on top of us, Mary eating my chest as I swallow her hair. When she sleeps she makes snow angels but I love it when she kicks me because I know she's there.

Sometimes I see Polly sitting Indian style on the practice green when we leave the golf course in the middle of the night. Or next to the car, staring through the glass at us fucking in the front seat.

I get better at ignoring her, start to like the fact she watches, until the night I look up and she's gone.

Mary says, "Why'd you stop?"

Mary looks like Cybill Shepherd if she'd never been young. Thick and blond and everything else blurred. But she can sling a blender at forty miles an hour. She can smash porcelain coffee mugs on your nose when you reach in a bowl to touch her fish. She can fill a sliding glass door, silhouette like a beanbag on its hind legs, and bitch about bamboo, or how she's addicted to ginger ale and Visine, or give me a birthday card that ends: *Since I've first known you I've always been proud to be loved and respected by you. Nothing's changed—Mary.*

Every time we fuck I hope Polly's looking. I watch out the steamed bathroom window for her floating on the siding. Get out of the shower and check behind the mirrored cabinets. In the toilet tank the puck dissolves in a whisper. Back in bed Mary snores and grows like a burial mound.

I cheat on Mary with a shark-faced Swede named Haber who's got toy hair and when you pull the string in her back she says the same thing over and over again.

Out on a small dock in December, snow drops in bright white pieces like the stars are crumbling. The lake is frozen, except in the center where it's smashed-up mush. Haber cries on her knees, in each hand half my zipper, which she just undid.

"I can't do this," she wheezes. "I like Billy. That's the only reason I'm out here," and runs back to her car.

Me with my boxers blown up in a sail. Way out, there's the hole in the ice, you can even see it in the dark.

Just having stood there surrendering my pants was enough for Mary to leave me. I knew it at the time. But now that she's left I miss the neuroses, the flying appliances. I throw wood chips on her window at ridiculous hours, wander toward her parking spot after school, to where she's circled her spit on the pavement in chalk and written my name.

Later, night's asleep behind the grocery store. No one answers beneath the empty stadium bleachers. No one drunk in the field in the rain, breathing my firecrackers. No cops in the dark parking lot, promising I did something.

From sheer indecision I wander into my twenties, into bars looking for Polly. It's like trying to stare a crack into plaster. Girls leave with their boyfriends and leave me phone numbers illegible under lipstick and the crush of the napkin. Or they circle the crowd like promoters, flirting up fights. I sleep in the open hatchbacks of random parked cars, wake kinked in the dawn from someone else's tire iron.

Years pass like this. Jumping in paper trucks from my balcony; asking out waitresses, cabdrivers, delivery women; falling in bushes and rolling down flat sidewalks.

Then someone wakes me up in a bar booth and tells me I'm twenty-six, blows a tiny horn in my face. She dances away from me, blinking glitter like scales, dancing between scattered tables and a long aquarium with its ticker tape of miniature fish.

I run home to my couch and the bottle I left there. When it's empty and spinning beneath the table I throw full beers out my window at a couple fucking under a picnic table. The next second and several hours later, in the blue room of my morning, I'm pissing in my own shoes and missing.

Then the dry cement of Saturday under my skin, my whole life standing on my temples. I swear off drinking even as I run to make the last happy half-hour.

It's dim as I thought it would be. Drunks joke their ashtrays, fly banners of smoke from their fingers. The muted made-for-TV movie with its jukebox sound track, the conga of bottles and teeth, each couple in its own cigarette soap opera.

My drink spills from the bottom of my glass. I spit between the stools, let it fall off my lips. It takes minutes. I buy a drink for the shadow in the corner. I tell the bartender, "The serious guy, underneath the smoke machine." He knew who I meant. But he never came back for my money.

I curse liquor until close.

*   *   *

But that Sunday I wake in a bed of beige playground gravel and watch the sky pass above me through the squares in a set of monkey bars.

A woman screams, "Kids, don't touch the drunk man!" with a voice like a whip or like it wishes one was around.

It's then I notice all the kids semicircled around me, as if just the nun screaming was enough to create them—kids born in noise, with jelly-stained faces, hair cut in shapes they can't control, navy turtlenecks and rainbow suspenders, corduroys, patched knees and NFL lunch boxes with butter sandwiches, communion wafers, holy water by the thermos. A girl in a satin jacket wears a green candy ring.

"Where's your sermon?" says a skinny white kid with black luggage beneath his eyes like he lay awake all night, waiting.

The girls laugh and poke their own cheeks.

I stand in the dome cage of the gym set. The kids giggle, stare and point, like I'm a clown priest or a penguin—Jeanie (says so in the satin) screams, "They ain't got no knees!" and she's right, penguins got no knees, but it's little laughing all around and she's talking about my jeans, knees bleeding through the rips.

I try to laugh too, only I puke on the monkey bars. Kids spray every way toward the church, screaming like a bomb. I haunt the playground forever. The nun is going to eat me, I see it in her face. I run after the kids, who screech worse until a few get trampled. One kid hits a tree, falls back with eyes closed and a plum of blood on his forehead.

I run faster, through the herd of children all falling dead to the gravel as I touch their hair. Some collapse just seeing me.

Even without the nun giving chase I still sprint two miles away, hit a low steel rope at the edge of a parking lot. I land clavicle first in a puddle and come to rest beneath a pickup.

And yet no one stopped me on my way home. No hysterical bank teller on the sidewalk, screaming in train hair and comfortable shoes, *Is he okay? Did you kill him?*

In fact, the mailman waves. The fat woman cranking a wrench on the fire hydrant asks if it's hot enough for me as her nest of children screeches in the middle of the street, bouncing with their eyes closed. Everyone I see winks. A man at the bus stop chuckles to play the jolly fat guy. My life has become a McDonald's commercial, red-and-yellow everywhere, the makeup still smiling. I deserve the one with the clown in the dumpster, you can see the red shoes from the drive-thru—the one where he shot a hole in his red wig and the manager found him in the bathroom, birthday party crying in the background because they can't break the Grimace piñata. I should stand among people wrestling in line and watch dogs bark at the fry cook.

I don't deserve these happy old women, sweating on their stoops eating jokes for breakfast. Or the newsstand man with the airbrush eyeball on his eye patch, all smile as he spanks the paper. Maybe I recognize only the end of things.

* * *

I get a job at the butcher so I have a reason to get up in the morning. Behind the scenes at the meat museum, one kid makes sawdust. Another sticks chickens on a spit, each neck up the ass of the next. I get a bloody apron and a white paper hat from some fifties soda fountain. Back where we work is raised like the pharmacy, with wide wooden tables and abandoned knives that can cut through bone.

Dancing on the other side of glass-shelved flesh and cheese, a white woman my age pushes hips toward prosciutto. She's got a skin-tight Morton Salt T-shirt. Haircut like a duck but it looks good and as I watch her jeans—crow feet in the hips—I'm happy I'm wearing an apron.

"Where'd you learn to dance?" I say. "A strip club?"

"Yeah," she laughs. "Strictly clothed of course. My friend's dad owned one and some mornings before he opened he gave us the stage. And we'd pretend. You know, use your imagination?"

She's dancing again, eyes closed and her hand in her hair.

"There's a song in the stink of the sausage," she says. "Hear it?"

I look around at the meat: the slice stacks, the thick steak piles, the hams hanging in their net-rope bags. So much flesh that, if you wanted to, you could believe it all was singing.

Man
in Towel
with Gun

I HAVEN'T SEEN A.C. SINCE SUNDAY.

At three-thirty Tuesday morning, drunk and learning Japanese on TV, I started really wondering where she was. I'd already learned *ta toki ni,* which was to say something like, *After an action has been completed.* Such as: *Heya O Deta Toki Ni,* or close, which means, *After she's left the room.* Usually she called, even if it's a "Fuck you, I'm over here" kind of message.

In the kitchen each tile whirlpooled within its edges. The dark counter bent at the waist, spine of drying plates. I opened the refrigerator. We keep citrus paint by the gallon in there because paint man told us otherwise the organic elements begin to deteriorate. "Then your walls stink for years," he'd said.

All three potatoes and our garlic aspired green stems. I threw them at the trash can and a few went in. I left the aged onions, lemons, and limes imploding mold, tennis ball peppers, tomatoes from the crypt. We had a spit's worth of ginger ale, whiskey in the freezer. Ice. A frost-coated swizzle stick. I've got what my high school guidance counselor called "the wrong motivation."

I grabbed the drink ingredients and something I hadn't noticed for two days—a poem instead of note she'd stuck to the freezer door with an anvil-shaped magnet:

10:45
Went to 7-Eleven.
I've sat in that chair,
watched two of myself dance.
Not owned my own
teeth. Felt where I was plugged in.
You want to know did I meet your green light.
Get your fucking
hands off me.

Okay.

See, we're both poets. She paints things too—chairs, walls, the neighbor's tricycle—some on canvas for class, since that's what she's getting her master's in. Mine's poetry, maybe I said that already. She paints from video stills, in pitch-dark except for the television, two flashlights trained on her canvas and a microscopic desk lamp illuminating her palette. Her masterpiece leans against the red leather chest in the living room: *Man in Towel with Gun,* one of her James Bond triptych she's since broken up. Somewhere else in the house hang the other two: *Henchman's Teeth Flash* and *Surface-Sealed Shark Pool.* You should see the way she lets light play off the carnivores. Still, her half-naked, dark and blurry, armed Sean Connery remains the best she's ever done. It's life-size, wide as a Ping-Pong table, keeps ripping its nails from the walls and falling on its face.

We met first semester and lived together ever since. Graduation's in a month. Both of our degrees and $4.50 gets you a fish sandwich, which is about how much we make each week teaching. You get to grad school to find out without a fellowship you earn your keep leading classes, the way you wash dishes in old movies when you can't pay for your food. In class I might've said, "Her use here, in the poem, of the *fuck* gerund resembles something like determination. Maybe she's coming back. Maybe she's got this, that, and the third to say about it. Do we, as readers, believe her assertion?"

Sometimes other poets come over to hear what we have to say, or sit in her beautiful chairs. Mostly they stand on whatever table she hasn't painted yet and read their own poetry in our infamous living room.

The week I moved in with her, A.C.'s naked friend puked from our window and the cops showed up. That was enough to seal us for good in most Master's Program minds: forever the oven heads, the lush rummies, the interracial sex freaks who'd do God only knows what if they got you alone. That was the half of our class who ate sweaters and sat in their apartments pushing dust through homemade mazes. One guy had a smell-blocker flannel shirt he wore around smokers, special gloves to handle silverware and candy bars. Once he found a hole in his sleeve and spent the rest of the night sniffing his arm, asking me, "Does my elbow smell?"

Everyone else hangs out at our place. We see every form of asshole ever conceived.

Dawn in my clothes and I've pissed the couch. Arrogant sun laying itself naked across the living room. Television still awake. On-screen neon leotards with people in them punch the air, bouncing on smurf-blue Astroturf indigenous to the cliffs of Hawaii. The ocean behind and below them in rows of teeth, waves and waves and waves to the horizon. I change the channel to a wide dry valley.

It says, "Once a great diluvial water course, not so much as a creek remains of it."

On my way upstairs the light sings and sways on the steps, stands worse in the bedroom, sweating and crowded, breathing everything toward the center of the room where I lie on the bed like a stain.

I wake up to Wednesday evening's hungover compunction, nothing from my window but hot gray, roiling across roofs. The rain-stained buildings have seen this day before, their entire lives spent wide-eyed and focused on whichever slim monster of a tree has been assigned to stand across their section of sidewalk. Each one staring straight ahead, ignoring the rest, whole neighborhood in the same train car.

I make my way around the house, yelling her name into empty rooms, closets, under beds and desks. The first Bond painting came from her *Men Holding Things* series, all of which lean in two stacks against the wall here in the den. *Big Nigger with Ice Cream Cone* and *Fireman Daisy* front the stacks, the only two from this period that'll make her thesis. The first title's mine: guy's got a light-blue shirt and a melting cone, stomach stuck out and a drip on his belly.

Our car's still parked on the right side of the street. Her friends don't like me so much, can't call them. There's the wine cellar, but we don't go down there anymore.

Her grandparents killed themselves a while back and left her this dilapidated brownstone with its useless cellar: row after row of ancient bottles, split corks, vintages ruined to vinegar. She'd lived here for years and never been down there. She'd imagined things: brains in jars, stockaded children slowly becoming veal. I convinced her to search it with me and those big flashlights, the headlights with handles. Every now and then we'd get lucky, find some sixty-three-year-old pinot noir and throw a two-person party. Most of the time we got reds so acidic they'd eat through cement and whites too poisonous to even dye Easter eggs. Eventually we quit trying.

Her parents we don't see, because a nigger's infesting the house, and they won't visit till it returns to whatever baseboard it crawled from. I was listening on the phone when her mom said that. It was Christmas, and that night A.C. and I sat silent out back, slowly getting drunk in hooded coats, holding drinks with gloves, her trying to smoke cigarettes in mittens.

I decide to go round Mooney's to have a drink and gather a thought. Irish pub with some form of green in every corner and a hardwood floor covered in long burns like someone went at it with a flaming hatchet. I teach tomorrow, but it's the last day of classes and poets don't take finals. Bartender just set a shot glass upside down in front of me, said next round's on her. Now we're cooking with grease.

I have my thought: *If I was an A.C., where would I be?*

Don't have a single answer for that.

The girls on my right have skin-tight T-shirts and slogans across their breasts: SLAP MY ASS, PULL MY HAIR and GET YOUR FUCKING HERE, respectively.

The middle-aged woman on my left has angels for sale, hand-crafted from fabric, pink paint and macaroni, magnets on their backs. A pair of four-inch Betty Boop Statue of Liberties for fifteen each. A stack of lottery paper and scratch cards. She knows all this DJ's doo-wop: she only has eyes, she sings. Looks like those dried-apple dolls posed on crates by the gate at the upstate cider mills. She's around eighty, or an old forty, telling me how to find my girlfriend.

She says, "You get that *guy*. You know. The one in them Agatha What's-her-face movies. Wore the derby. Turned-up mustache," running one finger in a spiral through the air above her cheek.

"The Belgian sleuth?" I say.

"I don't remember *what* was wrong with him," she assures me. "Just the mustache. He could solve the hell out of a mystery though." Pushes a thumb behind her ear and says, "They got guys just like him in the back of the paper. You could get one of them."

I agree. I buy a magnet and take her number on the back of one of her scratch&sniff-a-pair one-dollar-lost tickets.

Surprisingly, A.C. isn't in any bar I find. By the fifth place and tenth drink I'm thinking things like, *She always talked about moving to New Zealand.* Maybe I'll get a postcard from

Auckland in two weeks, *Wish you were dead, A.C.* Or she bused away for that Dakota lobotomy she always threatened. After threats she'd say, "Take me. Seriously." Maybe a post-surgery postcard: *WISH YOU WERE FEAR!!!!!, Loves.*

All the missing-person flyers on every telephone pole between here and there've been ripped and pissed on. Even the ones head-height. Whoever found the one-ear corgi answers to Skimbörd kept it. No one'll sublet the shared room, conveniently located b/w hospital and bus stop.

But the nearest park is filled with hippies in greasy jeans and thirty-year-old dirty Jesus beards that attach with real rope. Crowns of dead weeds and flower stems. Under the lights they drink wine in stomach-shaped suede can-teens. Or most of them—I see a guy with a whiskey pint in a white wax bag. And that Public Access freak with what-ever the hell in his thermos, a circle of skirted dirty-dread androgynies Indian-style at his feet, analyzing his hand gestures. A.C.'d pretend she was a hippie when convenient, depending on the party.

I sit next to her ex-boyfriend Carrier, a white guy in a mesh Rasta tank top who paints too, never wears shoes. Thirty-two and runs a juice bar so he can ply students with secret herbals that make them sleep with him. I found his number on A.C.'s cell phone twice last week. We press sweat into a bench. Carrier looks for the holes in his beard where his fingers go.

"I'm stayin away from the middle of this," he says. "Middle's no good. Doomed before you start."

A.C.'s told me about this guy. Fucking her from be-hind on a boat. First man to ever cum on her collarbone.

"You're in the middle already," I say.

"I dated her first," he says. "I'm before you. That makes you in the middle."

"Look," I say, "I'm just asking where she is. Either you know or you don't. You're like some plant I pass in a hallway. That I ask questions and it answers me. But you can't say it was coming right out trying to admit something."

"Yeah," Carrier says. "But sure."

"She won't even know."

"Oh, she'll *know*," he says. "She knows already. She got some kind of witchcraft and doesn't even know it." He's nodding, agreeing with himself, pointing at me. "You know it. And I know it. But she don't even know it."

The skirts clap. The Public Access guy has a head the size of a stadium mascot and everyone hopes he'll spin it around. The beard below his lip glows wet yellow in the street light.

"But I thought she did know," I say.

"She does," says Carrier. "We're talking about two different things here."

"She saw it coming, then," I say. "She wanted you to tell me."

Carrier scratches his eyebrow with the thumb next to his cigarette, smoke down his face.

"No," he says. "This is not it."

He squirts vodka into his mouth from a sport bottle he stole off a bike and passes me the liquor often. He also took a headband from the handlebars, has it bent up in his hay dreads, holding them back.

"I had a dream once where everyone was trying to stick their heads up the asses of these statues," he says. "Didn't matter if it was Teddy Roosevelt, his horse, or Jordan spread-eagle outside the United Center. The Lincoln Memorial." He holds up the number 1. "And no one'd ever gotten their head up Lincoln's, you know, since he's sitting. The point is the statues, and their asses. And that people wanted their heads—"

"I got that part. Then what happened."

"Hell, I don't know," he says. "I remember screaming things. Dead dogs in the gutters. They might've been asleep, mind you, but the rainwater should've woken them up I thought. And I was sticking to the roof tar 'cause of the heat, and I just remember thinking, 'That's not what I meant at all.'"

He looks in my open mouth, shrugs, and comes up with, "Just thought it was relevant."

Bugs bounce off streetlights in clouds of brown rice.

"You think maybe something happened to her?" I say. "Something bad, I mean."

"That's not what I said, but . . . Could be. Who's to say?"

"I'm asking *you.*"

"Yeah, but. Who's to say?" the bastard says.

Public Access is eyes-wide and whistling, leaned over, almost up off the bench. His hippie minions smoke cigarettes and clap with the other hand.

"I know you-all called each other last week," I say.

"So do I," Carrier says.

"What'd she say?"

"I wasn't home."

"If she's at your place I won't kick your ass."

"Thanks."

"I mean it."

"If I were you," he says, "I'd check over Sissy's house."

"She doesn't like me so much," I say. "What're my other options?"

"Stay here and see who gets their ass kicked."

I say, "You're lucky I'm in a good mood."

"Or else," he says.

When I buzz her apartment, Sissy comes down in a sleeveless dress made of paper. White girl, skinny as a toothpick bridge. She doesn't open the door. She talks through the chicken wire buried in the glass.

"*What*," she says.

"A.C. hidin in there?" I point up the steps behind her.

"Thought she lived with you," Sissy says. Her skin's damn near translucent, looking more like a newt by the second.

"She does," I say. "She did. She in there or not?"

"Depends who's askin."

I stand slightly swaying on her doorstep, look over both shoulders for other people.

"Me," I say. "If you were to ask me right now."

"I am."

"You seen her?"

"Couple days ago." She drinks from a mason jar.

"And she was all right?"

"How do you mean?"

"I just haven't seen her in a while," I confess.

"And?" Sissy says.

"Maybe something bad happened to her."

"Maybe she left," she says, like she knows something about something.

"She wouldn't just leave," I say. "Something must've happened."

Sissy's got her hand on an elbow and the drink against her forehead. She looks at me, says, "So in other words, you'd rather imagine her tied up in somebody's basement, getting fire-hosed or whatever the hell, than come out and admit she just *left you* 'cause you're a dick."

"Now who do you know," I say, "keeps a fire hose in the basement?"

"I'm done talking to you."

"So you think," I say.

She smiles a little and I remember she blew me once in a taxi. We'd promised to fuck in the future, like now maybe.

"I know what you're thinking," she says.

"No you don't."

"You'll never fuck me."

"So you think."

"You said that already," she says.

I watch her calves walk back up the staircase.

★   ★   ★

Sissy lives right by Columbus Circle so I go sit on a bench at the entrance to Central Park. Sometimes, like now, I'll come up from the subway and stare at the red neon A&E [**Biography**] sign, lying on its side atop that twenty-story building. Beneath the advertisement is a scrolling digital ticker—forecast, who's on—like a horoscope, or a fortune cookie, or a poem:

> **Humid**
> **Mostly Sunny**
> **Slobodan Milosevic**

or

> **Seasonable**
> **Chance of Showers**
> **Mary Queen of Scots**

I don't deserve A.C. She's intelligent. She can feel. I'm coated with wax. I bungle the subtle things. I mash tiny buttons five at a time with oversized fingers. I sit here and wait for tonight's verdict:

> **Sweltering**
> **Mostly Cloudy**
> **You Are Shrewd with Affection &**
> **Will Thus Die Momentarily**

I sprint sweating for the subway, spend the whole ride ill and trembling. No one'll sit next to me.

⋆   ⋆   ⋆

When I get home I turn on the television, wait to die or find out who's on the late-night *Biography* replay, whichever comes first. Only booze in the house is some yeasty German beer we got as a present, months old and hot in a top cabinet. I pour it on ice with a little water.

I'm still alive when the show comes on and reveals tonight's subject: Sean Connery. Figure I have to watch.

Born 1930 Edinburgh, Scotland. Son of a truck driver. Black-and-white photo of him as Scotland's entry in the 1953 Mr. Universe. He came in third. The salad Bond days. *The Untouchables* Oscar. The gray-bearded later years.

After the bio, I watch *Golé* for a while, a highlight tape of the '82 World Cup with Connery narrating. I shut it off when a tiny Argentinean buries his heel studs in a Brazilian crotch. The seventeen-year-old superstar gets sent off, and Sean says, "The world will have to wait for its new hero."

I wake up in a dry bed with sand in my eyes and wrenches raining through my braincase. Twenty minutes till my class. I can't keep doing this. Today I will not drink. I take a French shower in my sink, pick up the students' stack of crappy poetry, and run toward campus. Even with a shaved head I can still smell cigarettes in my hair.

I'm fifteen minutes late and the door's locked. I don't have keys. Whole class on the floor or bent over in the hallway. Kid next to the water fountain trying to keep the drip off his pants. Minnesota Jim jumps to the rescue, a blond chopstick of a kid who always wears sweater vests, the twitching, hermit crab personality of the congenital nerd, but acute, like he was the one accused of masturbating in the auditorium during lunch hour. But he's eager to help. Says he's friends with the janitor.

"Of course you are, Jim," I say.

This makes him happy. He sprints off.

I'm leaning back against a wall taking deep breaths, a cold sweat of pure bourbon.

"You okay?" Tina wants to know, pink halter and her tongue spinning on the end of a pen. Her breasts are wide and spreading their arms for a hug.

Jesus, what's wrong with me.

"You still haven't come by the Blind Pig," Tina says.

That's where she bartends. Twice a week for an entire semester I've had to talk myself out of going in there. She's done it all: miniskirts in the front row; offers for conferences at her house; suggesting we take everybody by the Pig for cheap drinks after class, then doing a shot with me at the bar, turning to face the room and placing her hand on my cock, winking at me and running off for the table.

"I'm not doing so hot," I tell Tina.

"I know what you need," she says, nodding and smiling with pursed lips.

"A shower and a nap?" I say.

Tina says, "You got the first part right."

Minnesota Jim comes bounding up the steps, shaking the keys, proudly holding them up like he's just pulled a baby from a well. I let him unlock the door and he nearly seizures he's so excited. As the class files in and the lights blink on, Jim's hopping up and down, the keys still raised in the air.

He's saying, "Teach! I just gotta take these back to Clarence! I'll be right back! And I gotta go to the bathroom too, so it's gonna take a minute."

I tell him to take his time. In class I tell everyone to think about the semester while we got a minute. We're waiting for Jim.

I excuse myself, grow gills and drink for at least five minutes from the water fountain without a breath. When I stand up—*head rush*—I fall face first into an art student's locker. She helps me up. She's very nice about it. Jim comes up as I'm thanking her. I say to the art student, "Do you know my friend Jim?"

Jim says, "No. She doesn't know me. Hey. I'll be in there whenever you're ready," and heads into class.

The class is an hour and a half long, half an hour now gone. Even if I'm in a shitty mood, whenever I sit in front of a class I instantly start smiling. Written on the chalkboard from whatever class before us: *THE COURSE OF LIFE As Three Parking Lots Seen from a Long Island Train: school buses, ambulances, garbage trucks.*

I assign a thirty-minute timed writing.

"You know that song?" I say.

I'm trying to think of it. My brain feels like it swallowed a brick.

Jim says, "So we should address that question in the poem?"

"'You Do It to Yourself,'" I say. "That's the song." I hold my hands up like an evangelist. "So there it is. *You Do It to Yourself,* and what the hell does that mean? Write."

After ten minutes, I go out to the water fountain, then all the way down to smoke a shaking cigarette outside. I try to remember what day it is and whether A.C.'s finished with everything yet.

A jarhead in a letter jacket walks by with his girlfriend in a holster, giggling in his armpit.

"Hey," I say to their backs. "Today Thursday?"

Jarhead shows me his profile and says, "All day, buddy."

By the time I get back to class it's turned into a forty-minute writing, twenty minutes of class left. "Okay," I say. "Who wants to read?"

Everyone suddenly takes notes on something. I could milk this silence for the rest of class, a couple more "Come onnnnnnnnn's" and some arrogant premed would stand up and finish the semester for me.

For some reason, I'm not in the mood for that. "What about yours, Jim?" I say.

"I don't want to read mine."

"C'mon, man, it's the last day of classes. Even if it's the worst poem ever written—and I'm *sure* it's not—you're a very talented writer, Jim. But what if your favorite writer, what if Burroughs said, 'I don't want to read mine.' Then where would we be?"

"But it's really short."

"And every midget actor could have used that as an excuse to stay home. Now come on."

He starts to read in his chair.

"No, no, Jim," I say. "Stand up. Come over here." I stand up myself and come around the front of the desk, sit on it, face the class, slap the spot next to me. "Up here."

Usually when they read in class they stay in their seats. If you're terrified, you can sit in the back so that when it's your turn, most people won't turn and look at you.

Jim hesitates in his seat, swallowing rapidly, running his Adam's apple in a circle like a rosary.

I nod.

He comes and sits next to me. He wasn't kidding— the poem is short, just two lines. I put my arm around him and say, "Read it, Jim."

He's holding his paper like he's got a butterfly by the wings. He stares at the back wall of the classroom and says:

"You do it to yourself.
And that's all there is to it."

No one knows what to say to that, least of all me. I concentrate on something stuck in my eyebrow and nod intellectually.

"Jim," I say.

He's got a look like I just came through the door with a lab coat and test results.

"Jim," I say again. "I believe you've just invented a new form: the cynic's haiku. I'm serious. That was absolutely brilliant. What'd you guys think? See, Tina liked it."

In the end they took their marked-up theses off the pile and waved their see-ya-later pleasantries. Next to the pile I'd left an appointment book open to let them know, in case anyone wanted to discuss their thesis criticism next week, hey, I'd be available. The only date and time filled in was tonight: *8:00, Tina @ Blind Pig.*

I come home to find the phone off the hook and the answering machine still lodged in the wall, blinking letters.

I shower for an hour, head downstairs in a towel to find A.C. in the blue glow of the kitchen's black-and-white television, bloodstained jumpsuit, eating a pint of ice cream with a fork.

She's got light-green eyes that liquefy your brain. Even in a dark kitchen. Curly neck-length hair looks like it rolled down a hill and fell on her head.

"What's that guy say in the movie?" she says.

I say, "Which?"

"'You shot an unarmed man.'"

"Did not," I say.

"Then the other guy says, 'He should've armed himself.'"

"Don't know that one."

"Yeah, well," she says, looking from my head to my feet and back again, "You should see it."

She's watching *Dr. No,* part of TBS's Bond All Week Long. Last week was the Squint for Clint marathon. Week before that, Crazy for Swayze. I watch the first Bond for a minute, hoping for a bikini-clad Ursula Andress, shell in each hand. Instead I get Dr. No angry at the dinner table, crushing a gold Buddha in his gloves.

"Is that *your* blood?" I say.

"It's paint."

"Where the hell've you been?"

"Here."

"How come I didn't see you?"

"I saw *you,*" she says. "Speaking of which, I hope you turned the couch cushions over."

"I don't know what you're talking about."

"Then turn them over now."

"Duly noted," I say.

A.C. waits for me to say something else.

I come up with, "Sissy said you left me because I was a dick."

"You are a dick," she says. "I just haven't left you. Yet."

"That inspires confidence."

"Wasn't meant to," she says. "And why would I move out of my own house?"

"Considering the situation—"

"Exactly."

"What about the note on the refrigerator?" I say.

"That's my new poem," she says. "Like it? Wrote it off the top of my head. I got talent for days." Endless insults slot-machine through her eyes. Instead she says, "I've been in the wine cellar. You know my thesis is due tomorrow."

I forgot she paints down there sometimes. I forgot she had a thing due. "So I guess you'll need your space tonight," I say.

"You got somewhere you can go?"

"I'll dig up something," I say.

She sets down the ice cream, picks up a mason jar of her own, rim thick with lipstick, jar sticky-fingerprinted. She must've snuck some liquor to the cellar.

"That's what I like about you," I say, tapping my temple. "Always drinking."

"You wish," she says, grabs my hand. "I want to show you something."

She leads me out into our back courtyard of apartment windows and high weeds, music falling—hip-hop, Latin house—screaming, fire escapes, silhouettes smoking and sitting at kitchen tables. A.C. opens the cellar doors, giant oak things made from the sides of boats.

A candle appears in her hand. She shows me the stone steps. Here are her flashlights. VCR on PAUSE. The work-in-progress on the easel's only an outline of a figure. "I just finished that one," she says, points in a corner. It's a variation on her masterpiece, an empty-handed, completely naked Connery with a shotgun for a penis.

"So see this," she tells me. She's got a great idea. "Even the ones I can't sell we hang down here," she says.

She says we could ring the walls, have our own gallery. A museum even. All we need are nails and lights.

But I'm looking at the old, buckling beams in the ceiling. The ones that say someday soon this whole thing'll collapse.

Quality Fuel for Electric Living

WIND PUNCHES THROUGH DUMP-TRUCK WINDOWS, SMASH-ing Pucker's voice to shrapnel, to fragments of scream from one foot away, his neck veins screwing spiral, alive—"LIKE IT SO FAR, ACE?"

But he could have said *spade,* so there's that, and I nod too quickly; get that white-hot wire-hanger pain in my neck, smoking like an omen. The dash says 8:13 in the A.M. and I'm already sweating; last night's whiskey still twitches in my stomach, biting at the lining. So dehydrated my blood feels like electric tinsel. "HEY ACE, YOU DON'T LOOK SO GOOD! NIGHT OUT WITH THE BOYS?"

"Well it was a night out with my girl, until she killed that and I went and got wasted by myself."

"BEFORE YOUR FIRST DAY ON THE JOB?" he says, and I'm ready for a first-day lecture when he says, "MY KINDA MAN!" and claps me between my shoulder blades like I'm his son, and I'm choking.

While I look for my wind on the truck floor he still screams as he drives with no eye on the highway. Wind-shield could be a sheet of lead and he wouldn't notice, this half-Canadian take on a redneck, STATE HIGHWAY T-shirt tight as a rash and sun-faded green—*Lt. Pucker* in cursive on his chest with the silk-screen rank stripes right on the sleeve. Heavy leather head like a sun-burnt purse, nose folded over his face.

His speech had started with some kind of invented headline like: GIRL TROUBLE GETS US ALL! so I'd stopped listening, but started again just in time to hear him say, "HERE'S A TELLING STAT ABOUT MY LOVE LIFE, LET'S GET THIS ONE ON SPORTSCENTER! PAST SIX MONTHS, ONLY NIGHT I GOT LAID AND ONLY NIGHT I PUKED BOTH FELL ON THE SAME DATE! HOW'S THAT FOR SHOWIN YA WHAT YOU'RE MADE OF? I DON'T LIKE THE DIRECTION THAT WEATHER VANE'S POINTIN, I'LL TELL YOU THAT FOR FREE!"

More and more he began to seem like the kind of guy you hear at a strip club saying, "I think she likes me."

Yet he's giving me advice, asking me questions like, How'd she do it? Why? How'd that make you feel?

"She dropped me over dinner," I say. "Like some kind of goddamn mint wrapper. She said I was a dreamer. Said I'd never become a chef watching cooking shows on the Food Network all day and then I said you know how many of those guys are self-taught? And she said but they still had fucking jobs and I said now I got one and she said well it's too late now. Plus you're a drunk, she said."

But Pucker's stopped listening so now we just drive. The nuclear Tonka rattles through the heat like it's reentry, down the gas-stained beige beltway on a pair of prairie-schooner shocks like a rodeo in a box; using our heads to beat itself a sunroof. Crouched drivers in sedans the color of families pass us, ears near the radio for rush-hour wreck news.

The truck CB blasts an hour of static through a second, loud enough to halve a skull, then, *"PUCKER! WHERE YOU AT?"*

Pucker quick grabs the handset to face like it's oxygen, "YEAH! THIS IS PUCKER!"

(He'll never stop screaming, ever, he'll scream for the rest of my life.)

The transistor again, this time two numbers at top volume, *"TEN FORTY-FIVE!"*

"WHERE AT?"

"IT'S OVER ON THIRD AND PEAY! BENEATH THE RAILROAD BRIDGE!"

My old girlfriend lives over on Peay and Sixth. You can see the bridge from her door. A month ago, when a high school wrestler hung himself from it and swayed gray-faced in the rain you could see that too. There were cops spinning the crowd around a ring of caution tape below him. Cops on the bridge pulling the kid up by the noose and wherever his feet swung the whole crowd moved, all with mouths open, hoping he'd break open and rain prizes.

Pucker screams his own two numbers, "TEN FOUR!" Returns the handset and sets his hand on my shoulder, stares at me with a speed smile, tight at the corners 'cause he's still not fast enough, "A TEN FORTY-FIVE, ACE! ON YOUR FIRST DAY!"

"What's a ten forty-five?" I ask, but the wind—and he changes gears as I say it—growls and grips the stick shift, tries to push it through the floor.

We're off the highway, among the filed-clean suburb's rich teeth white; lawns green as expectation. Aluminum huts in Lawrence Welk shades of sorbet—before pale cherry a woman leans on a mailbox, waiting on delivery. Her crimson sundress strains on her gut ball, fabric flailing a trail behind her like a comet flying in a standstill and she salutes to shade her eyes. She's alone on her mowed hope among the morning-car extinction of her neighborhood, gravid in red.

We're at a red light, and with the truck stopped the heat hits in full, the sweat doubles, pores gaping to ooze. I blow scent across the truck like a whiskey skunk.

Pucker's stopped screaming, still talks too loud, laughs, grips the wheel like he's ready to rip it off. "You smell like you're gonna LOVE this!" Dump trucks don't have rearviews so he has to turn around to look in the backseat as he hits the gas pedal saying, "Hey Mighty Joe, get up! TEN FORTY-FIVE!"

In the back bench a brother sits up, cranium expanding as I realize its size. The absolute, magnific, planetary mass of skull astounds; bone shouldn't grow that big in this gravity. His shirt's as faded as Pucker's but with only one stripe. *Pt. Joe Young,* the silk script label. He'd slept through the shocks on fifty-pound lime sacks, bloody gauze and clawing wrenches like robot prostheses, slept as if he'd been killed, or tranquilized.

"I SAID TEN FORTY-FIVE!"

Joe rubs his lids off to get the eyes open. "I heard you, man. Why you always be yellin." He puts his monolithic fists behind each head in front; ashy like he's been crushing rocks bare-handed. Taking up the whole backseat, got his legs through the bottom, running us where we're going.

We come onto Peay through a tunnel of trees, pull onto the gravel shoulder. A half block away the bridge runs over Peay, connecting two sections of forty-foot hill.

Right in the middle, wedged in the bridge's iron support, a dead deer hangs like a venison piñata. The cadaver's crooked neck looks at its hook, its tangled antler. Even from here I can see blood strung from its stomach to the road.

Pucker's hands sit on the steering wheel insinuating U-turns. Both he and Joe say nothing, give me time to realize that "ten forty-five" has something to do with the deer.

I try turning the truck with telekinesis.

Pucker busts the silence with, "How the hell the animal manage that? Well, fuck, I'll be back," and he's out the door, clank like a tank hatch.

"Hey Joe," I say. "What's a ten forty-five?"

"Animal corpse removal."

"Corpse removal?"

"*Animal* corpse removal."

We watch windshield television without volume. In the morning movie Pucker walks away from us, staring at the pavement like his eye fell out.

"I wonder what happens next," I think out loud.

Joe rubs his colossus skull somewhere around the back. "He'll think of something to do and we'll do it."

I turn on the A.M.-only radio and "Superstitious" scratches its way through Brillo pad speakers.

"No Stevie," I say. "Too early."

"There," he says. "Leave it."

It's talk radio: "*I cannot prove to the anonymous public that I have a legitimate relationship with my wife.*"

We watch Pucker below the deer, hands out like he's asking it why.

"You believe in signs, Joe?" I say.

"Pends on what kind of sign it is," he says. "You mean, am I gonna pay attention to NO U-TURNS at three in the morning?"

"No, like omens. Auguries. Forerunners."

"This about that girl?" Joe says. "The one dropping them mint wrappers?"

"Yeah," I say. "We broke up last night. She said I drank too much."

"No offense my man, but I could get drunk just *rememberin* what you smell like right now."

"You on her side?" I point at the animal. "She lives about three blocks up that way."

"No shit?"

"None. And you know what else? I'm startin to think she dumped me at ten forty-five."

"Now you're makin shit up."

"I'm serious. In fact, I'm positive."

When Joe's quiet I can hear his head hum, hear it bending metal, changing tides, magnetizing. Then he says, "What she say when she did it?"

"She said something like, 'Nothing ever changes until it does, and then it happens so quick you don't notice and it seems like nothing's changed at all.'"

Joe says, "The hell does that mean?"

"I don't know," I say. "But right after that she said, 'I'm here to tell you things have changed.'"

"Oh," he says. "I know what that means."

"Yeah, me too."

Arden also said she knew it was over back when we saw the hanging kid. She said I was instant elation and quicker disappointment. A clock striking one, she said.

But I didn't tell Joe any of that.

"How'd you hear that, anyway?" I say to Joe. "You were asleep."

Joe says, "You said it in my dream too."

Pucker crams his head in the window, "ONE GRENADE'D KILL THE BOTH OF YA, NOW LET'S GET TO WORK." He steps off the runner and holds his hands in his ass pockets like a third-base coach.

We step out on the side without shadow, truck still running and the radio on. A woman trapped in A.M. says, *"Isn't there something I can do to make it all just go away?"*

The three of us stand in the street in the heat. I'm in the kind of mood where the sun glows like God's burning anus and that kind of light hurts, like when the artist goes insane because his paintings mean more upside down.

I thought we'd be digging or something. I'd already pictured it, a van Gogh, right side up, *Spades with Spades*, me and Joe curled aboveground in dead-tree stances. Above us crows cracking in joints like living letters, over a cornfield, as we try to make a hole in the crust of the earth.

Anything had seemed better than that, ten forty-five a re-
lief. Right now, I want to dig.

"All right," Pucker says. "Mighty Joe. You go whack
that guardrail we just came over," and he points at six-foot
weeds bamboo-shoot thick, thorns like tomahawks.

Wish I got to do that. Hanging deer begins to feel
like my responsibility—

"And you," Pucker says, finger at my head. "You're
gonna like this!"

"Thought you said I was gonna love it."

"Might even," he says, laughing. "Might even." Now
he thumbs at me. "Kid's got a sense of humor. You know,
colored fella just quit last week had a sense a humor too.
Kinda looked like you, matter of fact. What'd you say your
name was again?"

"Nimrod."

Pucker laughs harder, slaps his thighs like cartoons
taught him. "How the fuck could I forgot? I'm sorry, I'm
sorry. Nimrod. Well goddamn."

He reaches in the truck and pulls out a four-foot
weed whacker, the evil steel-cord kind.

Joe smiles wide as a barn and walks away sweeping
the whacker in a two-handed M60 shake, strafing everything and the truck, cutting us in half.

"What do you think about harbingers, Pucker?"

He smashes his eyebrows together. "The actor?
Wasn't he married to somebody? Shit, let's go, we got better things to do than stand around with our thumbs in our
asses talkin about movies."

★   ★   ★

So the deer I have to deal with. Me and Pucker stand beneath it, watch it swing on its horned pendulum, blood spraying in the wind from an unseen stomach hole.

"All right," Pucker says. "This is what we gonna do." Shakes his head. "You gonna do. And stop looking at Joe. Joe bit this job in the ass a long time ago. Had to beat one dead with a pair of hedge clippers, thing was still jerking around. So this one's yours. You're the new guy, and that deer ain't going nowhere. That simple. Now climb up that hill, get out on that bridge, and see how that fucker got stuck. Then get it out."

He blows a piece of brain through a nostril. We watch hot cement melt the yolk yellow.

I squint at the deer. "How much you think it weighs?"

"Shit if I know," he says. "A ton."

"You mean a ton like two thousand pounds, or a ton like a shitload?"

"Both," he says.

"Bitch."

"Nope," Pucker says as he points, traces a hyphen in the air with his finger. "See, thing's got antlers."

I climb the forty feet of hill mud and hairy trash, among trees hacked up as knife-sharpened pencils. At the top, I'm sweating worse than ever and I wipe palms on my shirt for its first dirt. A black and blacker bird blows a holed song like it's got a nail in its throat. I walk toward the dead thing. Down the tracks, on dead wood ties buckling themselves from the inside out.

Now the bridge before me: wide milk green, with bird-shit whites and blood rust patches as if it's been buckshot. The sun comes off the green bright enough to stagger me. This goes on a hundred yards, maybe twice that. From up here I can see Joe off in the guardrail of horrors whacking Herculean weeds; then the yellow dump truck, glaring like cartoon margarine; and last, below me, Pucker blowing poison darts through cupped hands, or just screaming, sound delayed as starlight, "WHAT'RE YOU, JACKIN OFF? THE DEER'S BACK HERE! THEY EVEN PUT A LADDER DOWN FOR YA!"

And they did. Right next to the slightly spinning corpse. I put my hand on the ladder rail, watch the ground lower below the deer.

The ladder shakes like a house drain and I watch every metal mesh step. Loose screw shavings stick to my head; even looking down I get one on the tongue in a rusty communion. Then the deer smell hits, comes in its own wind: sweat on dead, dead in sweat, and I look at it, stare it right in the eye fats, the edge-headed swelling pupils, the deep sea green and no land in sight, no blink, a permanent expressionless pause—we're a photo of someone alone, waiting for a person who never shows up.

"KICK IT IN THE SKULL TILL THE ANTLER RIPS OUT!" Pucker screams.

Which sounded specific. Too specific. "Hey," I say. "You put this here? Some kind of right-of-passage bullshit or something?"

Lima-bean-size flies with deer in their teeth head-butt me, bite my back through my shirt, yell at one another in chit-zipper voices.

I try a headlock, deer ear on my neck, and I start wrenching the head back and forth. The neck's broken—bones knock like a bag of rocks, grinding themselves to pieces.

Pucker says, "IF THE ANTLER COME OUT NOW, YOU'RE COMIN DOWN WITH IT!"

So I stop. Pound a fist on top. It thuds like a hay-covered rock.

"C'MON NIMROD!"

"All right! I'll fuckin kick it in the head!"

I crack my weight down with a boot heel and still get the hay, still the rock, but now you can hear a hollow. Skin starts to rip up like wet grass.

Joe's in the truck, moving the bed in position for the fall.

Pucker yells, "WHAT'D YOU STOP FOR?"

"The skin's ripping off!"

"AND?"

So I kick some more, same spot, till the skin's gone and I'm slipping on flesh, meat starts to shred in my treads. I gasp, heat choke hold on my throat. A dry heave knocks my head into the ladder.

Red aggression burns out my pores with a gasoline smell and I start stomping skull until there's a bone-patch bald spot, a glaring wet white shine, a crevice—only a thin line, but hope—and with a jerk and one more heel the horn breaks off with a crack like a plank smacked in half.

Joe and Pucker run from the truck and the falling meat bomb.

Slow, the deer turns, tries to have its head hit first but only makes it halfway. The force almost hops the truck off the ground. The stomach blows open, blood from every corner of the deer, eager to pool now that it has a container.

"Coal train!" screams Joe.

And I like that—"Coltrane!" Like "Goddamn!" "Jesus!"

"Nimrod! Train's comin!"

From the ladder I look downtrack, train rounding the trees. Whistle howl so loud my brain shrinks. I rattle up to the tracks, turn to run and see: down on Peay, three blocks away and standing outside her building, what looks like Arden, kissing somebody who's definitely not me.

"YOU BIT—" I scream, but the next train whistle slaps the rest out of my mouth.

The train's coming full beds and *fast,* blowing carbon through the trees like volcanic ash—a transportable coal explosion, trying to shake itself off the rails, rattles into another dimension. Solid-rock windshield. The grill pulls its lips back, snarls forties' industry and a wartime mind frame.

I'm at the edge of the bridge now, looking back at the noise makes my eyes bleed—the coal-spraying breathing machine, spiked with hooks and hand grips, switches and couplings. Things to latch on to, take you places. I stick my hand out.

When it's almost close enough to grab I run away, smash shoulders into blunt pencil trunks, get the back of my head pelted with coal. I hit a wood fence at the base of the hill, lie on my side to watch the train pass, listen to the motion of the wheels: "stackcorpses stackcorpses stackcorpses stackcorpses." On maroon sides, white said and repeated every bed: QUALITY FUEL FOR ELECTRIC LIVING.

Pucker and Joe above me; Joe squatting, staring into something's burrow in the bottom of the hill.

Pucker says, "You almost ent up like that wrestler kid got his head cut off by the train."

Joe laughs into the hole.

The train whispers something about distance. One time, from atop an ottoman, Arden said I made everything look difficult, but it was really just me. Like a midget playing piano standing up, with no bench, she said.

We head back to the shop, deer in the dump truck. About my love life Pucker has this to say: "Get yourself some strange wolf and you're right back on the all-star team." Joe doesn't say anything. We're swimming in afternoon midatlantic beltway, an entire traffic of confused Floridians searching for Pennsylvania.

My zipper's broken open, blood on my pants, wet in the pockets.

At the garage we park the truck in a gym of a spot, complete with brick walls and a partition; rim and no backboard, thirteen feet high. Pucker's already dragged the carcass across the parking lot full of crooked-parked pickups and hatchbacks. You can see the maroon blood smears on the asphalt, tiny pieces of hide stuck in certain people's fenders.

Me and Joe get to hose down the truck: the earth off the side, the clippings off the tires, the blood and intestines out of the back.

I stand on the cabin with the nozzle set on firehose, shaking a pitchfork in its rack. Joe's somewhere near the undercarriage. He's got Arden advice too: "Fuck that shit." He says that's what he'd do.

Truck cabin open, talk radio still falling from the door speakers. I stop hosing to listen to some guy go on and on about ghosts—theories, sightings, definitions—"*A residual haunting effect or energy left behind by a traumatic event. A murder-suicide, for example—something sudden and violent that for some reason has imprinted itself on the fabric of time and space and will sometimes be replayed to people as they pass through the area where, uh, these people met their demise.*"

Joe peeks his head out from under the truck. "You hear that?" he says.

"Unfortunately," I say.

"Sometimes," Joe says, "I swear to God, I see my fucking aunt in my kitchen. And her ass got shot years ago."

"Who shot her?" I say.

"My uncle."

"Where?"

"In my kitchen." His wide head sweats on the cement and that wood sled he wheels himself beneath the chassis with.

"What's she do when you see her?" I say.

"Just sits there," Joe says. "Stares." He watches his wrench as he turns it in his hands. "Sometimes she shuffles cards."

"That's it?" I say.

"Sometimes she says, 'You're shiftless.' Sometimes she's not even there. Still, she's there even when she's not."

Pucker's crossing the lot from way off, dirty in his belly and sweating on his shovel.

This hose blows it all off—the skin and bloody hair, the larger chunks of organ, everything, not counting these stringy pieces hanging from the door latch. Or those lumps caught in the gutter's teeth.

Chimp Shrink and Backwards

ABACUS CLACK OF VERTEBRAE BEADS WHEN I TURN IN A CHAIR, spinal cord in a phosphorescent red shiver. My organs sleep on top of one another. Lungs reach for ribs, warm against the rest. I hear my heart walk slowly, smack heels on a flight of stairs. I feel all the soft hardware run uninterrupted, without clicks, whirs, gas, batteries, bytes, chips, bolts, pain, or smoke.

I'm black and I own a black suit. Wearing it right now. Wear it on skin on muscle on bone around fluids and crap that covers what I felt a minute ago. Black shirt. Black tie can't be seen, people think I'm not wearing one. The cops call my build athletic. Heard attractive before, who hasn't? Everyone's found attractive by someone.

Across the table sits Joan talking.

The place around us is tin-can architecture, a cylinder, a whirlpool of tables around a round stage in the center. I sit where the beans used to be. Disco decorations clutter the dark ceiling like dead satellites. Everyone black, everyone smokes, the bar curves around the back. The stage in spotlight, lighthouse in a deep fog, the thick poisonous kind that scares the sailors in the shiny yellow rain gear holding splinterwood steering wheels with hands that sting from seawater.

I look at Joan again. She's black in a black dress and she could be better-looking than me. Face long and carved into a warrior's mask.

"You're not listening to me," she says somewhat slowly, as addressing a foreigner.

"No," I say. "No I am not."

She looks across the room, down at bony fingers that tap the tablecloth. Her hand jerks like a leather spider.

"Goddamnit, Simon." Almost a whisper, her voice rolls around in a pocket. Now raises: "The only couple you're capable of is you!"

Her mouth held smaller than usual. Right eyebrow bent.

"Conversations aren't one side over the other. They're supposed to be expressions of possibilities." She says something else. Something about monologues.

There's a poet onstage, thin like pipe sculpture, a dark-skinned ivy brother, even bought the costume: Bill Cosby sweater, Popsicle-stick color pants. He wears glasses for personality.

"An original piece entitled 'Washing the Furniture.'" He says *warshing*.

Begins. More feeling in his reading than his writing ever had, behind it even he doesn't care. Bad posture. He sways in hula-hoop hip slow motion, drunk because he heard it gave poets a bad name.

"I knew a bitch name Cunt Mantrap," he says, swaying still. "And she was a *whore*!" He laughs occasionally; the words "dig" and "me" bounce on the floor in brand-name letters that fit right in your wallet. His lower lip pulls speech off the bottom of his teeth, flicking Italian hand abuse as he reads. He points while he talks. His forehead folds. He launches small spit particles that blink in the light.

"Simon?" she says.

"Simon?" she says.

"Simon!" smacks her palm on the table, rattles the fork and knife against each other, spoon left lonely.

"What?"

"God," she says to me. "You're worse than a chimp."

"Why do you always bring your work into everything?" I say.

At work she talks to monkeys with her fingers, watches them bang blocks of balsa with heavy rubber mallets. Watch twenty, watch a hundred, watch a thousand monkeys; one beats *Macbeth* into the air on a wooden square. They run around, smile long bone, signal touchdown, hop, shake things. She shorthands character traits. She names them. She says she's a scientist of the psyche.

Joan has been talking, reciting a list poem I've heard before. "Like picking dead skin off your feet when you're on *my* sheets in *my* bed. I never see you pick your feet when we're at *your* house. You won't even let me fucking eat toast in your bed."

"I—"

"Shut up," she says.

I grab edges of our round table like a bus wheel, door-lever calluses bleed the smell of smacked gum and armpits. I clench my teeth and settle in for silence.

Joan faces me, watches Pipe Sculpture poet with disgust in the corner of her eye. His current poem is jokes about fucking.

Weight surrounds my table. Minutes of noncommunication. Pores in our tablecloth expand. Ice melts. Food ages. Around me people change position with a *shish* like they're made out of corduroy.

A tall black man in an all-tan suit passes us through the water darkness, self-satisfied. At a table on the other side of the stage his date sits alone, staring at Pipe Sculpture.

I turn back to Joan. She looks still to the stage.

"Yeah," I say. "I got to go to the bathroom."

I stand up. She is behind me. I slip my crotch between shoulders on the way between the chairs. No one blinks when I pass.

Through the crowd, the bar distracts me in a fifty-yard curve. Two bartenders man twenty yards of filed booze sitting on glass shelves; the remaining shelf space runs empty along broken mirrors with a million fractured reflections each. I lean on the glass bar and look down the row of belly-ups, the row of other places' regulars, drunk soloists with their freedom and their liver problems. They sit on stools that turn and drive drinks into their teeth, wait for the end of the night. They fell through the crowd of round tables pinned to the floor with couple weights, crashed stomach first into the back.

"Help you?" a bartender asks me.

"Jack on the rocks and a glass of water."

"You know, we sometimes have seven bartenders behind here," he says.

"Is that so," I say without enthusiasm. I have ways to make people stop talking.

He rests his chin on his chest, dries a glass, and speaks softly. "Just not tonight."

Pours my drink in the glass just dried. Forgot the glass of water.

Parts of the bar are broken also, foot-long sections spiderweb in white shatter lines. I step across the carpet, listen to the ice bells chinking in the liquor.

I arrive at the bathroom, door squeals because it has to. Lime green walls like a meat locker I read about, white from here feet down to the black-and-white-checkered floor. Sweating urinal silver. Yellow crack cheap sink with rust drips beneath the faucets. Chipped paint claw marks stripe the stall doors. The light fuzzes perception, hums buzzing. The tall man in the all-tan suit stands with his back to me, with his hips square, legs slightly bowed, one foot in front of the other, poses dumb gunslinger. Suit custom made. Bought it with money I don't have. We both glow in the soft whites like aging-actress close-ups on television.

He has the black head of a grasshopper: compound eyes, large, oval tops pointing slightly toward each other. He admires it in a full-length mirror. Confidence keeps him company.

He grabs his lapels with the thumbs, an astronaut. Adjusts the jacket. His lower lip and chin is a section in itself, moves like a dummy, like a proxy.

"What do you think?" he says. He turns around, my jealousy replaced with veneration.

"That's a hell of a suit," I say. I mean that. "It's khaki."

"Not sure I follow you young man," he says. "It's tacky?" Glowers with the lower section.

"No, no," I say. "It's khaki. Like tan. I mean, it's nice."

He nods, sizes up my suit, considers a comment. "Ah yes. Well of course." Turns to the mirror, grabs his lapels again. Looks at himself at a three-quarter angle. Wipes sleeves with his arms straight out, telling me to steal third. "They call it the café au lait," he says over his shoulder. "Armani, you know."

"I did not know," I say. "How can a guy like me get a suit like that?" I ask.

He turns and smiles with the low section pushing the upper. Looks at the floor.

"I'll show ya," he says.

He starts tap dancing. Humming. Singing an occasional word, words. "My love . . . Around . . . To see ya . . ." Arms swing in front of him in mocking pendulums, legs snake around and across each other, feet spin in vibration. *Tippity-Ka! Tippity-Ka!* Loafer morse on the bathroom tile, he tells his life story to fingernails melting behind the radiator. I listen too and I hear it, the tapping always there, sometimes it fades a little and I can hear his orgones.

Still taps. Wipes sweat from his head with a bony middle finger or something else—four of them, wiping. A separate audience of automatic dryers shine fifties-car optimism from a foursome on the lime wall, reflect around his sideways face in fidgeting fat buttons of fender glint metal. Grasshopper grunts, twitch, soft-shoe Grasshopper. He slows it to a smooth finale, shuffles three times sideways, stamps his left foot on the floor in conclusion.

"That's a long story," I say.

"Follow it step by step and you'll be in my position some day," he says. "Suit and everything." He takes a last look at his head in the mirror, walks toward me, pats my shoulder on the way past. Heads for the exit.

"What about women?" I say.

"They feed you crap and expect you to shit steak, boy," he says to me. "They got *everything* backwards."

He waves with the back of his hand on the way out the door.

The door squeals closed, imitates itself in opening again. Grasshopper head pokes into sight.

"It's just that," he says. "*That*," points at my navel, intending to mean the whole suit. "Makes a bad impression on people."

I look down at my body.

"Understand?"

"I think so."

He nods, leaves. I hear the door again.

I admire myself in the mirror with a tan suit reflection. Three-quarter angle. Grab my lapels. "Not sure I follow you young man."

Walking now on the carpet in darkness, it looks navy, purple, brown, black like blood, maroon maybe. I look up in time to the see the row at the bar all drinking, winking at me without looking, like they're my pops, like they understand things, all things, cauldron blisters on their fingers from the witches of their past. I turn to the swirling crowd and, centered in a cone of light, raised on the stage, Pipe Sculpture reads a blow job poem.

"Blow me on me in me in you you on me it jussss-sssst keeeeeeeeeps commmmmmming."

I tack through the crowd and again no one blinks, busy with the back and forth hissing of small words. My table slowly approaching. Joan still watches the stage with a face of impending spit.

On the opposite side of the stage Khaki Grasshopper sits with one knee over another. He raises a drink. *Understanding what needs to be done,* he doesn't say.

I sit down, raise return.

He laughs hard with his low section, smacks the table.

Across from him, his small date slumps depression. She smiles when he points at her, resumes her previous activities: napkin fold, fingerprint wineglass, sigh flares shot toward the chandelier.

He points at me now, still laughing, winks a compound eye.

"Who's he?" Joan asks me.

"Nobody," I say. "Just some guy."

Mouth held smaller than usual and right eyebrow bent return to her face, never left, always there maybe, like the sweater she's wearing, same maroon as the blood pool carpeting. She wore it the first time I saw her, walked through the crowd at the man-made lake fixing her bra strap and she never meant more.

"I have a question, Simon," she says. Whispers her interrogation, "Do you know what I do for a living?"

"Yes," I say. "You are a psychologist of chimpan-
zees."

"No, Simon," she says. "I'm not. That was over a
year ago. Remember that one month when you were woken
up before noon every day because I didn't have a real job
either? Did you think I was just skipping work to help you
find something?

"I—"

"Chimp shrink was the first thing that ever stuck in
your mind and you haven't paid attention since."

"But—"

"No," she says. "No but." She grabs her side of the
bus, looks for the blue route signs, *make the drop-off polite
like.* Rolls her finger around the rim of the wineglass. "I'm
an animal trainer now. I train chimps for the movies. You
could've guessed that, Simon. After all, what's always been
my lifelong dream?"

Years of conversation at a glance, high-speed micro-
fiche, overhead transparencies, Post-its, planes dragging
nylon letters, crystal-clear images of high school textbooks,
the theory of photographic memory.

"To have twin boys?" I say.

She puts her elbows on the table, rubs her eyes with
the butts of her palms.

"No," she says. "No, that definitely was not it. It's
to be in the movies, Simon. That's the answer to the fucking
question."

Pause, looks at me, bites one thumb in silence, close
to breaking the skin.

"Well," she says. "At least my goddamn chimps'll

be on the screen. What the hell've you done, Simon? Huh? I'll tell you: Shit." She holds it in the air two-handed, like a postcard. "Shit is exactly what you've done," she says. "You're an English major who never graduated and I'll tell you something else. They got a name for people like that, Simon. And it's *a fucking bum.*"

She hasn't been drinking. She puts the bus in fifth. Catch your stop on the fly.

I'm not getting off. Grab metal bars by the door, never served a purpose before. In the undermowed lawn next to her bus stop, there's a dead black Nova, weeds growing in the seats, a knotty pine fence the same weathered, stained white as a hundred years of piss on an inbred's crooked teeth, a couple slats missing. Loneliness sitting alone as a pit bull bitch, white body tattoo-stamped like a cartoon suitcase with marine slogans and beer logos, writhing at a chain, hanging herself in horizontal leap jerks, bust the chain when I step in the bus stop, canine canines all along my flesh, pain as opposed to death.

"Well, Joan," I say. "It's the whole situation. Nobody's read the books I have and I've never heard of the books they've read. Not to mention the timing," I say. "Yeah, the timing. And the monetary issue."

I say other things I don't know the meaning of.

"You know what I mean, baby? There are things I got going on. Things I can't control. Things I *can't* control."

She doesn't hear me. She doesn't care. I'm not listening either, my part of the conversation is a formality. The words keep coming.

Somewhere toward the ceiling I see flaking rust on the bolts that keep spotlights from smashing poet skulls. I watch myself from above, an absent talent in the bad-color shaky film of my teens, when every word was a birth. Days spent searching for speech through a dirty attic brain of dust-covered donkeys and dinosaur frames. Stuff needed cleaning, step over look under, stuck, nothing, resort to the construction mud-boot words of everyday conversation; they sit in the closet next to the door mouth. Everyone has them, uses them. The sound they make is *clumpf.* Now the search is left unbegun and I fling boots out the door without effort.

Joan listens to the sound of humans sitting. To everything else in the room. To the stage, filibuster finishing, "You're a little cunt just like the rest of them! Thank you!" To Grasshopper cough from across the stage, people's low babel, man in the back clap three times.

Pipe Sculpture poet walks off while no one pays attention. Takes his place next to the rest of the poets in a line of folding chairs.

"Just shut up for a minute, Simon," she says.

A woman takes the stage, rolls across in folds, in unfolds, stands straight. Shaved head beautiful, thin, dark-skinned. Tall in a blue dress, she colors the light. I'm sure she used to high-jump. No atom cage of grief around her, yet the poems are grievous. Maybe she met somebody. She reads eulogies to herself but she's ecstatic through the middle with a flagpole spine of perfect posture. Her head spits her colors and I love her like a country. She could make me do anything. And now she points in no direction.

She speaks, "Open to show with your dirty nails. Who put the thumb in your brain, Erebus ersatz?"

Silence.

Joan clears her throat. Her mouth begins to move. Fade back to black silence of alley corners yet to be constructed. I can still see the poet, sometimes talking.

I look back to Joan's painted-mouth spasms. Her lips extend and open and slide across in seafloor mannerisms. At the bottom of the water, spread across miles of Paleozoic parade grounds and darker places where fossils swim around with dangling headlamps, are creatures like her lips, mouthing her words to the top of the waves. Sound becomes a record played slowly backwards, fits like a helmet: water in the ear, deep slow vowels for seconds, short hisses. *Zup. Zup.*

From right to left her volume returns, firm now, constant, in the middle of a sentence: "To think about me. What you do is not enough. Look around you, Simon. We're not satellites."

Cold craters in blue rock orbit.

"I bet you don't even remember what I ordered," she says.

I don't.

"You know what I think about a lot?" she says.

I don't know that either.

"What *I* want. I didn't used to do that, Simon. Like when we first met. Remember?" she says. "The man-made lake?" she says. "That's not me anymore."

She barrels the bus between houses that start looking familiar. Bus stop blocks away—I can see it. She can't wait for formalities, door hiss construction boot to the chest.

"It's ooooooooooovvvvvverrrrrrrr . . . ," her voice red-shifted in slow motion. I'm out the door in a Nestea plunge toward the tarred-together.

I see her face. I see her foot, her mud print on me. The bus side too blurry to read, exhaust ball, bus back reading, IT COULD BE YOU! Hear a chain break. I smack the macadam. Bounce. I lie and melt. Hold my grated head together. Bleed. I hear claws on concrete, barking getting louder. Loose rocks burn holes in my cheeks.

Dog pads skid to a stop and I can hear her tattoos standing over me. She hot-pants on my neck, aims slobber into my skull cracks. Eyes on my thighs and she's drawn away. Bites halfway through my leg, muscle safe in jaw force furious shaking feeding shark-headed demon pulls, she pulls, she pulls until it gives with a snap like a bridge cable. She chews. She swallows. She hacks up hamstringy pieces. Bites the other one and pulls, she pulls, and she pulls again and tears it in half, the rest rests warm on my calf. She walks into my sideways sight, yawns a bloody dog smile with a mouth full of muscle pulp. Jumps over my head. She heads back to the Nova, bowlegged strut with blood on her chest.

"Did you hear me, Simon?" Joan says. "Did you hear what I said. We're done."

"I heard you the first time," I say.

Onstage, Flagpole Poet wraps up. "Sliding the back side of time, the past is shit. Underneath, none of us matter. Belong. To anything. But ourself."

The entire can stands in ovation: claps, stomps feet, whistles, screams, shakes the picture. Khaki Grasshopper looks confused. Pipe Sculpture sulks and scowls at the

other poets. Flagpole walks offstage slow, succinct, smiles
through the noise in a crown. She's convinced the crowd
to be more like her.

"Why aren't you saying anything?" Joan says.

"I thought the conversation was over," I say.

The two men who said who went sat fat by the
front and the coat check, the smell of wet wool and wire
hangers. They say a woman won't be last; being last is
important.

Stand By Poet stops pulling on his cigarette, turns
metal gray like his chair. Thin already, loses weight instan-
taneously. All set to go home, thought he had an excuse,
grabs his belt to hold his pants, makes for the door,
stiff-arms Sheila (who organizes the readings, clipboard,
bolt-straight back, stands at the end of the poet row and
knows she's in charge). He makes it to the coat check
where the two fat men jump off stools to grab him by the
throat.

Sheila sprints through the tables screaming, "Don't
hit him in the face! Don't hit him in the face!"

She weaves through chairs dropping clipboard pa-
pers on the floor. "Do you hear me! He's on next! Don't
hit him in the face!"

One fat man hits him in the face. Fat Man #2 in
a sweatshirt too small—his bottom belly sniffs a moose
nose over his belt. He beats repeatedly on Stand By's
chest. Hear moaning bursts of pain from all the meat in
his body.

The men drag Stand By to the stage. He limps to
the microphone a stern joke, moves like beef jerky. Stand

By's life has always been day-old bread in a fat baker's shoe tread, seventh in a six-pack, February 30. Now, here, a lifelong quest in the happening. He has the face of four elementary-school classmates never remembered. Body the height of a human, nothing unusual, noticeable, freakish. Dressed in denim.

He bleeds internally, coughs into his hand; motes float in his head gravity. I forget him as he reads, voice evens out into a dull smooth dial tone slides through my brain in a see-through slide show; words appear.

"I would," I see him say, "murder my*self*. If I were stuck with you. Only, I'd die slow. Painful. Make sure at least *that* would be interesting."

Joan left the table and I didn't notice. I know that because Grasshopper sits where she was, stares, reflects me in a million mirror chambers for each oval eye.

"Where's Joan?" I ask.

He drinks vodka cranberry, smokes handrolls like a girl. "If you're talking about the person who was sitting here," pulls tobacco off his tongue with a hand or something else, looks at it. "She's on her way to the bathroom, with all the other women in this goddamn place."

This is true. All the women make deliberate for the door in a suppressed rush. Joan in front. They zig between numberless tables, zag around chairs. Put their hands on the backs on the way past, warm from the woman just left.

Some of them pause, take a knee like they lost something, serious profile against the now curtain side of a tablecloth, let a few women pass, then up, zagging again. They file stoic around the stage, quiet as S.W.A.T. A couple wear blood-pool maroon sweaters and they never meant more to me either. A few leave as couples. Their backs in coats, backs in dresses, backs in backless dresses, jagged lines toward the doors.

Stand By notices nothing. Everyone sitting watches him.

"Why are they all running out the front doors?" I say.

"I told you," he says. "They've got it backwards. Like to make things harder on themselves." He laughs to himself. Tan suit folded into a hard sharp line at the knee, like cardboard. "You should certainly know that by now, boy!"

Now he laughs loud square noises on my face, slaps his knee.

More words appear from the direction of the stage: "Mary had a little dog. So I ate it. We were in a fight, I mean, you would too, right?"

"They'll be back?" I say. I think of the backs before, shoulder blades bending skin from behind.

"Sure." He drinks, sighs with a wet lip. "Maybe."

"You ever done this before?" I say.

"Oh, absolutely. I'm a regular," he says. Bug smile fades. "I read here once." Rolls a cigarette in his lap, slaps tobacco from a suit fold. "They didn't . . . appreciate it."

"They ever come back?" I say. "Tonight, I mean. The women. They ever come back?"

His hands around a new drink dropped by a waitress who slides away before seen.

"No," he says. "But that doesn't mean they won't."

He drinks, throat pieces move to make way.

"No," I say. "No, it doesn't."

His face odd-shaped, being insect, his eyes glitter black lake rain.

"Let me tell you something," he says. "When the sun explodes, all that's left are the insects." He drinks, gasps at the liquor burn, signals distant waitresses for another round.

"We have to worry about that?" I say.

"Everything is a possibility," he says.

Stand By continues to read to a half-empty room. Voice slides slower now, some squares blank white, some upside down, some gone too quick. An occasional sentence crammed onto one, read fast: "Andpersonality!Ratscanhitapelletbutton,I'mnotimpressed."

Around the room men sleep with their heads in their arm laps, others, head back, mouth in a hang. Stand By continues, no longer words, just white light and a deep hum lapping, lapping, lapping against the walls, the doors, against the bar in back where all the belly-ups are smiling. Against my temples.

My eyes are half open. Across from me, Khaki's eyes don't have lids, open while he sleeps. He nods without consciousness, neck snaps, drools on his hand or something else, on his suit, on the carpet, dark without color.

Everything's that color. I can't see.

I Got
Something
with Your
Name on It

HEY,

I got something with your name on it. Stick with me.

Remember before they turned on the carnival? All the folded rides, dead lights. That white kid from the funnel-cake trailer, one used to suck his toe at the pool. One always singing, "*I'm so full of ideas, and here is the good one.*"

Yeah him. You know Troy. He gave it to me. Said you might need it. Had it in his trunk in a Hefty bag, under a roll of orange electric cord and some lumps of bloody butcher paper. He had funnel cakes—stacked in paper plates and packing tape—told me forget those, said they wouldn't travel well. He was on his way to a bus, a barbeque. Told me if anyone asks, say something like, "Ain't seen him long as I can remember. Wouldn't know where he is." Say something like that he said.

So here it is. If no package accompanies this letter, call me. If it's been opened, interrogate mailman. If none of this means anything to you, I don't know what to say.

Troy said meet him in The Rusty Scupper parking lot at such-and-such a whenever. I pulled up and he's already there, sitting on his fender with the trunk open. Had these rubber gloves on to hold the garbage bag. Huge ones, blue, kind for industrial dishes, radioactive food. And he was real anxious, all jumpy on strings. Handed me this stiff thing wrapped in brown paper. It creaked. He wouldn't let me put it in my car. "Not right after I just handed it to you," he said. "Take it inside, they'll think it's a birthday present."

I said, "Who?"

"Whoever's watching," he said.

Now, I don't trust Troy as far up his ass as I could put my foot, but I went and had drinks with him anyway. Turned out perfect: The Scupper nearly abandoned and Cheri bartending. Our glasses never made it half empty and she gave us all the misorders: squid rings, monkfish, fried appetizers. Troy massacred the buffalo wings, only an oval plate of bones left. We got fake lobster-claw fortune cookies made out of shrimp toast. He threw me one and ate the rest, paper so greasy it was see-through. Every time I looked he was reaching between stacked plates, trying to get his fist in the hush puppies.

I did what he said, held it against my ear like a present.

I said, "A sweater?"

When I went to set it down, Troy didn't want no package on his stool. *No package. My stool. What if a woman wants to sit here.* That kind of thing. He was deep in the tall-glass flamingos, rum punch, and schnapps, red syrup on his lip—I mean ugly—drunk and swollen, puffed up like that science teacher they fished from the lake. Dead and bloated next to the paddleboats.

Speaking of science class, remember Kara Underhill? I don't. But I got an email from her saying, "Sorry missed you at the reunion. Sister said she saw you, I'd love to hear how you're doing?; I'm two kids and married. How didn't

I see you last winter? At the Wizards game, you still going out with what's-her-face?" and on and on and on. Coming out of nowhere expecting me to give a damn. What if I don't remember you? Or do and don't want to. I think she wants to get down. I might if she's who I think she is. Didn't you?

Troy was pretty sure *he* had. Yet he couldn't remember what she looked like, who she hung out with, or how old she was. Then he lit into you.

No idea you-all knew each other that well. He told me about when you two broke into the movie theater in high school. Selling E at football games. He told me a bunch of shit. How much you scammed off those two bookies went to Howard. And how they found out right around the time you fucked off and split town for college. How he was the one who got duct-taped in a trunk and thrown in the Potomac. He's still pissed about that.

Anyway, don't castrate the messenger. I'm helping *you* out. Even if this is a houseplant, better you than him. I mean, Troy might be cool and all, but he's like thirty. When you sleep with a minor *and* her mother, something's wrong. C'mon, one or the other. Self-centered as a bisexual. Not that that in itself is surprising. Didn't he kiss somebody else's girlfriend like six homecomings in a row? Won't find that record in the yearbook. Guinness maybe. Right next to his *Most Times Left Back, K–12.*

He used to drive to Driver's Ed and park his Jeep on the sidewalk. Banged the teacher. Said he did, anyway. Think her name was Lina, Leah, Tina, Ruth? She had at least a thousand shades of homemade crotchet dresses and always the same dirty slip. So beautiful it was painful, for her and for us, you could see when she squinted. She showed movies with animated highways that said things like "Stay away from wolf packs," or "Yellow = Slow Down," and she'd laugh, since we all know it means speed up.

Is this about Lorelei? The package, I mean. Maybe you haven't looked at it yet. Hope you don't still talk to her. You know she started fucking Troy right after you left. When she was still working at Bennigan's. I guess after that, too. Yeah, definitely. 'Cause when she started renting apartments I heard she'd take him to the empty ones, the ones nobody wanted. For months, nobody. They fucked in those.

If it's broken, Troy threw it on the floor. I shook it but didn't hear any pieces.

"Don't make me," he said. Hand kept slipping off the bar rail.

So you're not coming back. What's it been. Eight months? A year? Two? Got your address from your mom at the grocery store. The new one near Discount Liquor.

May not be my place to say but she looked like shit. I was worried. I mean, she's a beautiful woman. Could be I haven't seen her in six years. She looked weathered. I heard separations age people. She had luggage under her eyes, wouldn't look at me. Right in the middle of the spice aisle— kept shifting side to side like she was waiting for something to crawl at her from under the shelves.

When's last time you talked to her? She okay? Caught her at a bad time maybe. I have my days, weeks. I know how it is.

And what's up with your brother? He still in D.C.? Getting ass when chicks think he's Hispanic—papi this, papi that—I can see him now, nod and raise an eyebrow in a wrinkled Guyabera. Take them round his place to watch movies, pour some Mad Dog over ice, move slowly from kung fu to porno. Case closed.

Then there's you. How's New York? Get any? Heard it's dirty. The city, I mean. Then again, you get that many people in one place, shit accumulates.

Troy went to the bathroom and never came back. Only took me an hour to notice. I checked the toilets: empty stalls, clogged drain in the floor, window open. Smell like a saltwater slaughterhouse.

I came out of the bathroom to cops huddled around the bartender, talking plays—*Pump fake and go long*—all three trying to touch foreheads. This other cop talking into her shoulder CB. Then they were all looking at me, Cheri pointing. She said, "Where'd Troy go?"

I said you could find him in the water closet. Everyone found that interesting. The cops went and checked to see if I was lying. I grabbed the package, paid, and skated.

Anyway, that was last night, and I'm sending this now. I've already heard two detectives on my machine. One was a Detective Justice. Nearly shat myself it was so funny. I had a flight once and the pilot guy's name was Captain Divine, I shit you not, and when we landed everybody clapped. Sure it was a rough flight, but that's his job right? Nobody claps for the trashman. Look at me getting all emotional.

I called Lorelei about twenty minutes ago, see if maybe she knew what it was, but she wasn't around. Her sister doesn't really talk to her anymore either. You know Sam? 'Course you do. There's a nut job. Not like I'm telling you nothing you don't know already. She told me this story about Troy throwing Lorelei down some steps when he was wasted and then *immediately* launches into something about her neighbor bending over for the paper and how that's what she's looking for. Not just the haunches— Sam's word, "haunches"—but the guy cares. Apparently she could tell from just his ass. Hadn't talked to this girl in Jesus Christ I don't know how long and next thing she's giving me therapy highlights. She's quoting. I said, "I'm just looking for Lorelei." Sam said, "Wait, this is relevant." It wasn't though. Just more about masturbation and stuffed animals, rocking her crotch on her teddy bear's nose.

I don't know who else to call. The only other person'd be Cheri, the bartender at The Scupper. But she doesn't know Lorelei all that well and I'm not going back there anytime this afternoon. Or tomorrow or the next day. She doesn't start work till eight anyhow.

Cheri'd said something similar, except in her version it was Troy throwing Lorelei under a minivan in the parking lot. She heard she'd skipped town.

Give me a name and I could find out. Or you could call Lorelei yourself I suppose, if she's still there. Like I said before, I hope you don't talk to her, so I hope you don't know where she is either. Troy's on a bus, maybe he knows.

I'm thinking about doing the same—hop a bus and get out of here for a hot second. Cops make me nervous.

I'm talking hide for three hours in the basement 'cause you saw one at an intersection kind of nervous. Point being, I got friends in Connecticut and maybe I could pit stop by your place. That's why I sent it Express Mail. So call me. Call me whenever, or sooner. Even if this never shows up.

If there's no answer, no machine, then I left already. Maybe Lorelei'll beat me there. Maybe Troy shows up and we have a party. He did spell your name right. You listed? Hope not.

I'm kidding. No way I'm going anywhere near your place if Troy might be there, so you won't hear shit from me. Unless my friends don't live in Connecticut anymore.

Troy also said something about always wanting to see New York—"Skyscrapers and everything, just like I pictured it," he said. He said his friend told him they got three-wheel bicycles in New York, one's horizontal so you can't really get your feet at the pedals, but still, it's New York.

That'd be a trip, everyone together in when's the last time, if ever? Fuck a party, it'll be a reunion. Mac and cheese on paper plates and waving the flies off the beans. Just make sure you got booze—I don't know how long you'd-all last without it.

So heads up. Don't worry, it'll be fun. Then when the cops come you can have a shoot-out like Butch Cassidy and The Sunshine Band. Maybe you could borrow one of Troy's guns.

Whatever you do, make sure he knows I sent the package.

I never looked at it, case you wondered. All the peeling tape was that way when he handed it over. Plus it's probably had a rough trip. Felt like an adjustable desk lamp you ask me. Without the give and it made more noise.

I'm just glad it's out of my hands. I don't think it's a bomb or anything, else it would've gone off when Troy slammed it on the ground.

Motherfucking phone again. This place is like a telethon. If I knew any crippled kids I could make some money.

Anyway, sit tight. Like the lobster claw said, "Everything will now come your way." So if there's a knock at the door, you know who it is.

Thursday the Sixteenth

SHE'S GOT SQUARE-TOED KNEE-HIGH CYCLE BOOTS THAT make her look cloven-hoofed and Nazi. She pulls her skirt out of her ass—she's always pulling her skirt out of her ass—looks over her shoulder to check her work. Sometimes for a distraction she'll throw her blond hair around like she's mounting a motorcycle, when all she's ever really doing is exactly what she does every night: leaning her softening elbows on the black marble bar rail, whole scene framed in shiny fake mahogany like it folded open from the wall in a yacht suite.

I work here as a host, as in parasites, completely irrelevant and expect management'll figure out any minute now. Occasionally a rich midwestern couple wander in lost from the nearby airport hotel and my presence seems to make them more comfortable. People like that enjoy having their table chosen for them, if only so they can laugh, disagree, point to the table they really wanted. Always feels like I fucked up the card trick, or that festival guess-your-weight game.

We run local hip-hop, bad R&B bands from all across the nation. Weekly specials with ingenious names like Freestyle Friday or Dancehall Tuesday Night. A day-care happy hour where kids get to lick cigarette butts they pick off the floor and watch their parents suck face with strangers. If they're lucky the alcoholic invalid shows up and inside of forty-five minutes he's doing donuts in his electric wheelchair, his seeing-eye shepherd wandering among the drunks with a sign around its neck: DON'T PET ME, I'M WORKING.

Bouncers pace up by my host podium and hang their weight one-handed from ceiling pipes, swaying like apes, scratching their backs against doorjambs.

I'm second in command, behind Rusty the owner/manager/cokehead, if only because I found him his best connection yet. I get a lot of say in this place. Get to walk around, not walk around. Get to lean on a bar end and watch Casus stand in her cycle boots.

She's got a forties gas-stop pinup figure, healthy in the hips and chest. Brothers at the bar tell me how she looks even as I can see her twenty feet in front of us—they circulate behind me unseen, drinks singing ice and glass, held in football fists. They say things like "She big up top, *and* she keep a good waist," or "She got a big backyard, big backyard, look so good I wanna *rake it!*" Which made sense when you looked at her 'cause she'd definitely grabbed seconds at the ass handout, and used her extra helping as a weapon. Whole outfit offensives strategically focused around its firepower. Comments continue, some more direct: "God*damn* baby, how you fit all that shit in that skirt!"

Her name may be Casus but the official title she wears around the bar is the *Old Girl of the Cat Who Plays Here on Tuesdays*. They've been done for about a week. He left her for his growing pool of groupies and a short local fame, fat as a high school newspaper.

First Tuesday since they broke up and yet she's here.

Her ex Ollie's come up to the bar for his prefinale three White Russians, watched over by one of his big nigger football friends. Calls himself Ollie Ranks, or maybe Shabba Ollie, I forget. He's a skinny bald Trinny who always wears sleeveless mesh half-shirts, has a habit of plucking his nipples in the bar mirrors when he thinks nobody's looking.

He leans on the waitress station, ashing in the bartender's cut fruit. Ollie's so dark he has to wear gloves to eat Tootsie Rolls. Tattoo on his shoulder you can hardly see: homemade, done by a cousin fresh out of prison with a ghetto needle play set. It's a lion's head, years old and blurry to the point of looking like a shar-pei.

I point at it, say, "What's your dog's name?"

He says, "What the *fuck* you talkin bout?"

Onstage Ollie's band attempts to break something down. An eighty-year-old steel drummer bangs a calypso solo, white dreads hanging to the handlebars on his walker, spray-painted in green and yellow and red stripes. Next to him a sixteen-year-old dread-to-be, thin as a pogo stick, bouncing hands on an amped Casio.

Ollie's got milk lines down his chin, glowing in the black light like something subterranean. This used to be the time when Casus would have her hand on his ass, moving it only to pull her skirt out of hers. Or she'd rub her crotch on his leg and pretend she was dancing. Now he's got a groupie gripped by the back of the neck, his tongue pushing through her throat like an arm.

From halfway down the rail I watch Casus stare at Ollie, who might actually lift the girl off the ground if he doesn't stop soon.

One of the bouncers sliding behind me says, "Hey Theo, man, put yo move on, my brother, she be liking light-skinned niggas too."

"She just like *niggas*, period," but he's not around to hear.

I walk down next to her. She makes a face like she swallowed a fingernail in my general direction without looking at me.

The bartender is a rail-thin Egyptian, pointed nose, face like a ferret.

"What do you want?" he says. "You're working."

"Coke. And give her another of whatever she's drinking."

She says, "You come up with that all by yourself?" but she still doesn't look at me.

"Nope. I got it from Ollie."

She looks at Ollie. He's removed his tongue from the groupie's innards to watch us and he's no longer smiling.

Casus turns to me, smiles, bites her bottom lip, rolls a black earring stone between her fingers. "A drink *and* a smart-ass comment about my ex-boyfriend sounds like an approach."

"You're quick."

"All right," she says. "I've seen you in here. Working. So I know what you look like. I've seen the way you talk to people, the way you carry yourself. So I know more than that. I know enough to describe you to somebody, but *you* came up to me so *you* do the work. Describe yourself."

My first thought was to say, *I'm fascinated by insanity, war, and monkeys and think they're all related more than we admit or realize.* But I didn't let myself say it.

I say, "You ever heard that song where the lady says, 'big-black-monsoon?'"

"No."

"Well like that."

Old Man Calypso is done playing, mops the back of his neck with a sky-blue cloth, and sits bent over, dread head caged in his walker bars. The kid still plinks keys on the Casio over the premade computer beats.

The bar fink comes back with her drink and actually makes me pay for it.

"That's what I like," she says. "No fizz and you can smell it from an arm's length away."

Fink says, "You better get back to work before Rusty sees you."

"I am working."

Ollie discards the girl and grips the bar sides like he's holding the whole place still. Beneath the rail Casus takes my number.

I don't receive hers. I will be contacted with rendezvous location and time if operation still a go. These are the dating tactics of the gestapo high command. No names will be exchanged over the phone; we'll meet at "twenty-one hundred" instead of nine; and not *at* the destination but at some prearranged neutral site—maybe the park on 23rd, small as a doll house lawn, one arthritic bare tree like a fat gray weed—to give us enough time to slip our tails, cut through alleyways and door cracks in brick wall backs. From the kitchen into the dining room, we will emerge.

And that happens, all of it, including the twenty-one hundred, the meeting, the park. Except the emergence. But something close.

Now Ollie lives livid. Casus doesn't come on Tuesdays anymore. She comes with me now, on off-nights. And when I work Tuesdays I see Ollie squinting to see me at the back during songs. Old Man Calypso gets longer solos to make time for more Russians with even less white. There are slurred finales now, audible phlegm in the back of his "Buyaka!'s".

He spends more time at the bar the rest of the week too. When he's not dry-humping groupies with their heads against the tap beer, he's drunk solo—hanging off the waitress station, staring at us with his neck swaying. After a week he gets worse. Now he says *slut,* spraying spit in girls' faces.

I'm sick of his stare, his *slut,* his mesh, and his Caribbean belligerence.

One night we're in Casus's efficiency, the wet papier-mâché gray walls slightly buckled, some visible fault lines, like the inside of a cardboard box with a kid sitting on it. Walls bare except one, mounted with a ten-point buck head. Same wall holds the only window, but up in the corner so you have to stand on a stool to look out.

She says, "I hear he's getting worse. I mean, I can understand The Grava Men once a week, cause they're *from* around here, but Ollie's the only other one playing *every week*."

The thought plays a poster in my head.

She says, "It's time for a change. Fresh blood. New perspective. All that shit."

"I was just thinking the same thing."

She wears sweatpants, and in fact never wears skirts around the room, just hops in them on the way out the door. Maybe the skirt pull's part of her act, maybe she even clenches sometimes, makes her own opportunities.

"You could say something to Rusty, couldn't you?" she says.

"I could and I will."

Three P.M., empty bar, Fink behind the rail. He never left, he lives in the mop closet in a cage lined with swamp-yellow newspapers. One second after they let him out he begins cloth-drying glasses, his little ferret fingers flying over pints like he's polishing a nut. Even if ferrets don't eat nuts, this guy ate nuts, of that I have no question. His nose twitches as he polishes, mouth moves side to side beneath it.

Up onstage flashes the light test for the night set, blinking on the brick wall. Blue/yellow/magenta on empty instruments racked in skeletal metal at the foot of the drum fortress.

I pass Fink and the lights on my way to the office and knock.

"Yeah! *What?*" Rusty says. Got his name from his steel-girder red hair. Through the door I can hear him do a bump of coke, hear his head on the edge of combustion.

I open the door coughing unnecessarily, since everybody knows what he does, and sometimes he'll walk out with a chunk still caught in his nose hair. The first thing I see is his thick wood desk, wide as an elephant autopsy table, notched on the edges like an outback blade rack for the tools to hack up the animal. His palms down on the desk, ring on every finger. And higher up, the head swaying above his shoulders like a parade float in an inflated oval. His eyes have jagged red diagonals pointing at the pupils. His skin swims across his face in complexion weather patterns. Sweat staining his shirt collar.

"Hey, whaddup Theo, what's the haps, what's going on, what's the dilly yo?"

"You all right man?"

He sits up quick.

"*Yes.*" Looks at his left hand shaking two inches from the desk like patting an old man's head on the *Benny Hill Show.* His rings ring, bang against one another even though his hands bloat from the cuffs, dirigible digits pinched at the upper knuckles. He slaps the left hard against the desk.

"*Yes!* I am," he said. He slaps his hand again. "Coffee!"

Coffee my ass.

He looks side to side, at me; says in a lowered voice, "And can you smell the intensity, brother? It's coming out of the walls in this goddamn place."

"So I guess that guy's stuff works, huh?"

He pops his upper torso atop the desk, holds my shirt in both hands, faces six inches apart, "Tell me you can't smell it?"

I can't, but I can smell sweaty ring metal and a stench coming off his red head something like gunpowder.

"I can't smell a damn thing, Rusty," I say.

He lets go. Stands with cupped hands in front of his face holding an invisible bowling ball, mouth open. Falls in his chair.

"So? What? What is it? What's the thing? We're *in time* right now. Right this minute. Know what I'm sayin, my man? Know what I'm sayin?"

"I know what you're sayin," I say, *But do you know what you're saying?* "All right, here's the thing: I'm thinking we get a new act on Tuesdays. I mean, Ollie's good and all, but *every* fucking week? People been comin up complainin on their way out. Sayin they want a change."

"You mean, like, fresh blood."

"A new perspective. *All* that shit."

He leans back, folds arms for a photo pose in front of his car.

"Yeah, yeah, yeah, I think I'm seeing what you're meanin right about now . . ." Swivels in his chair to a grease-spotted white paper box atop his minifridge. Reaches in, grabs a handful, pulls out a fist of black cake dusted in white sugar. "Powdered chocolate devil's food cake," he says. "Help yourself, chief. Best thing in the world."

"I'm all right."

He puts a fistful in his mouth, opens his eyes wide, and doesn't chew. He leans over and lets the whole piece fall out of his mouth in the trash. "I'm not actually hungry right now, either."

"So Tuesdays."

"Right. And what are we doing again?" He's trying to shake cake off his fingers.

"Well, since I hooked you up, you hook me up. You know how I feel about Ollie."

That name gets his attention again. "You know he puked on the floor last week? Hold on a second." He licks his palm and wipes it on his pants. Picks up the phone, dials.

"Yeah, Ollie please? Ollie! My man! Here's the deal, bro, we're not gonna use you next week. Nah. You know, we need a change, fresh blood, new perspective. All *that* shit. You know how it go. All right, man, well, yo— give a homes a call, my man, know what I'm sayin? We don't hang out enough."

He hangs up, shoots me a side-headed wink.

When I step in her place, I can still hear the bell from the phone hung up hard. She watches me in the door.

"What?" I say.

"Nothing," she says. "Credit cards."

She walks over, pulls my T-shirt collar aside, kiss

biting to make my skin darker. Twenty-six and she's still
into hickeys. Never on the neck—on the collarbone, nipple,
hip, she leaves marks where they can't be seen. I *always*
prefer to leave the teeth out of it. Each time she bites harder,
I expect her to come away chewing.

I look at the ceiling, say, "In the bar I was thinking
that, you're a big girl, you know, and you affect everyone
around you just by being who you are."

She steps back, looks at me like I just shit on her floor.

"I meant big in a good way," I say.

She paces back and forth before her dresser, hands
behind her back. From the waist down she stretches a pair
of jodhpurs covered below the knee by the usual boots. The
boots almost never come off; she wears them during sex and
gets dirt all over the sheets. Her jacket tan like the pants
with padded shoulders begging for epaulets.

"Sit on the bed," she says.

I do what she tells me to. The buck stares at the wall
cracks, incurious, antlers touching the ceiling.

While she paces she holds her right hand in the
number-one sign, bounces it hard on the air every third
word. "Did you rectify the Tuesday situation?"

"I did."

"Good," she says. "Just like you were supposed to."
She stops pacing, turns to me on the bed, number 1 pointed
at my head. "Someone stopped by for you."

"Here?"

"Here. He left you a note." She pulls the paper from
somewhere, maybe out of her ass, starts pacing again, staring at whatever wall she walks toward.

The note says: *Never send to know for whom the bell tolls, it tolls for Theo.*

"What'd this guy look like?" I say.

"Had to be at least seven feet tall. Huge guy. Leather jacket. Monkey on his shoulder."

"I mean the face."

"I didn't see, he had a monkey on his shoulder."

I stop smiling.

She stops pacing. Looks at her watch.

"Six-thirty. Time for you to go to work."

At work there's no Fink, but there's a thirty-eight-year-old black lady, with NICI carved in her gold tooth, who pinches my ass when I bend over the bar.

"One of these days, boy, you and Nici gon have a nice, lonnng talk," she says and smiles, smacking her gum in huge clanking open-mouth unlatchments.

A bouncer throws out a drunk on crutches for walking funny. It rains so hard no one is here except a couple couples. Onstage there's a hippie hip-hop group with two six-foot lavender lava-lamp columns on either side of the DJ. All the lights they use are blue or purple, flashing slow—better to see the lamps, the empty tables, the couples not paying attention. Then the lights come on and the four-member audience leaves.

I carry stacked stained tablecloths to the closet, food in the folds. The bouncer's back from hauling trash. He's a swollen round white guy who introduced me to the term "donkey punch." Sometimes when he's silent you can hear his brain trying to work with an electric air pump's high-pitched wheedling.

"Couple dogs fuckin in the dumpster," he says. Puts his hand on the back of his neck, wheedles, waits for a response.

"Hum," I say.

"Yeah, so like, I put the trash on the side and shit."
He likes dogs, shoots cats.

"What if they eat the trash when they're finished?"

"They won't man. They'll be all tired from fuckin. You should've seen it yo, they were going *at* it!"

He walks past whistling Big Daddy Kane.

I follow, ask Nici if she needs anything else.

From across the bar comes a big, "Nuttin but you, Big Boy," saying "but you" like *Buttchew.* "Come on over here!"

"I, uh, gotta catch . . ." I say. "I'm meeting . . ."

"You gotta *what*?" she says. "Catch a *beating*?"

She yells out other things I can't hear on my way out the double doors you have to use your shoulder to open. There's thirty feet of concrete from here to the curb. Casus's car pulls up under the streetlight, a black Ellipse like a leech, with a walker strapped to the trunk. Back windows tinted; her driving, Old Man Calypso asleep in shotgun. What the hell is he doing in her car at three forty-five in the morning?

She hits his arm, grabs his shoulder and shakes. The two of them stare at the inside of his door and she points at it. He moves his arms around. She says something to the backseat. Finally Calypso's window opens, then the back door. Out comes a brother at least a billy club taller than six feet, with a head like an anvil. He's got muscles jammed in every inch of skin, trying to break out like too many potatoes in the panty hose. Even though tonight's cold enough you can see your breath, he's got a T-shirt says ONE LOVE—ten sizes too small—and a look on his face like he'd eaten whoever he took it from.

Ollie comes next.

He's got on a mesh tank top and leather gloves with no fingers. He's bleary-eyed and smiling, teeth glowing yellow.

Takes the next guy a while to fold himself out of the car. He's at least a billy club taller than the Potato Hose and cut monolithic: a stack of obsidian bricks. Wears a black leather suit with no shirt on, turns back into the backseat and pulls out a spider monkey, size of a big puppy. Obsidian holds him in his fist, four fingers wrapped around its rib cage. The monkey dick points at me and it pisses like the Obsidian's squeezing it out of him. The monkey screams mean, stares at me. He clenches and unclenches fists in front of himself, like it's choking an invisible turkey.

It's beginning to snow. I see events already laid out in boxes next to each other, inevitable as a calendar. No matter how hard I try to run back toward Sunday, Thursday the sixteenth will happen anyway, and I don't even have to be there.

I say, "Watch the monkey, watch the monkey. I could bust you for statutory ape or something, you keep *that* shit up." Shake my head, "What some people do to their pets, man, that shit ain't right."

The monkey goes still and silent on Obsidian's shoulder. The four look at one another, realize they're all out of the car, leave the door open, and walk toward me. The monkey doesn't walk, it sits. Even with wet left from P.M. rain, with A.M. snow sticking, sticking as I watch, the sidewalk looks harder than usual. Even the cracks look painful. I can hear dogs behind the bar, barking at their post-fuck trash feast. They'll jump back in the dumpster when they finish.

Sitting in the window on the other side of the car, elbows on the roof, is Pogo, even though you could never fit a fourth person in the backseat of that car unless you stuffed him in the marsupial pouch on the front-seat back. Pogo smiles at me. Three apes in the car, one in front of the bar, and the last four primates pant in the cold.

I watch them breathe while they cross the world's longest thirty feet: tiny monkey puffs; long gaps between the big brother's breaths; Ollie's even slurring his steam. Potato Hose punches his fist into his palm like a cartoon bruiser.

Over the shoulder without the monkey I can see Calypso asleep again. Casus leans across his lap.

She says, "Wait. Ollie. Don't," loud enough for me to hear but without the effort, like she's counting to three out loud.

Then she sits straight in her seat, kicks a Bavarian square boot up on the dashboard; lights a minicigar and holds it over her head to Pogo. Turns on the radio so all of us can hear and she changes the station.

The
Children's
Book of
Victims

HE SET OUT TO WRITE THE BOOK. SEEMED EASY: RECORD, then sort. No shortage of material.

Nine-year-old pushed in front of subway because the guy "just felt like it." Child, three, falls between train cars. Stroller carried off in closed doors, smashes on the tunnel exit. Sixteen-year-old dies in cold sweat at Broadway-Lafayette: dehydration, heart murmur.

That's four on the subway and I've only just started, he thought. Do adolescents count as children? The editor will no doubt care about such things. She might write "Means?" in the margins, red-ink arrows implicating specific sections. She might make him change the title.

Certain people might pick it up, look at the cover and think, Do I want to read this on vacation? This'd be the editor's point, as she stared at his proposed jacket: close-up face of a voodoo doll, stitched X eyes and blood on its chin. They'll think, Is this the sleeper everyone in my Hampton's time share keeps talking about? Is book club this week? What's Oprah say?

What if the author was some anemic kid from Janesville, Wisconsin, the physical manifestation of tin can and string? How'd that bear on airtime? If a journeyman sex-freak power forward wrote this book, would it automatically sell more copies? Why write anything if a meat neck with a few title rings could do it better?

Do it for the kids.

Who said that first, Ringling? The Cos?

Crib death up 300 percent in Harlem. Images of still-borns, unrecognizable messes of miscarriages in mop buckets. Americans spent more money last year on fast food than higher education. How about Duke Ellington spinning in his grave, but with a beat you can dance to?

The editor'd say, "Now you're talking book sales." She'd smooth the Band-Aid on her cheek covers a boil that's getting down right uppity.

The frozen runaway in a Dumpster. The intentional tractor accident. Girl throws newborn from boyfriend's window. Infant killed by puck at Rangers game.

This could go anywhere. He took down 864 more, ended with *The forgotten kid in the trunk,* and took a break.

He rented a room from a woman he never saw. She slept in the next room with the TV on sitcoms and every five seconds laugh track came through the walls. It didn't always manage the happy-fat-people sound they were hoping for. Sometimes it was more like eight surly teenagers, drunk in a panel truck.

His own television was the size of a football helmet and kept it going nonstop on mute, so he could look up and see baboons with the caption: [*SCREECHING CONTINUES.*]

She'd leave notes taped to his door complaining the bath mat was too wet, or about "uncomfortable pieces" left in the toilet. He'd write back that the bath mat might've been him, but he always flushed twice. Sometimes they left messages on each other's machines. Once every three months they'd startle each other in the kitchen, all two-sentence small talk and wide smiles.

They had revolving roommates in the third bedroom: the gay Croatian, the ladies' man fresh out of JuCo with half a degree in communications, the middle-aged cracker coke head taking dish inventory at seven in the morning and scurrying through the night around your room like a squirrel in the walls. They only ever stayed a couple months, but there was always somebody you might have to meet, talk to.

He crept to the toilet, no one in the living room. Smelled like someone had cooked steak, or maybe reheated meat. The smoke alarm chirped without batteries.

He had to hold the lid open, the synthetic navy fur cover crusted at the hinge and wouldn't stay up. Bottle caps and incense sticks sitting in the bottom of the bowl.

He looked at himself in the mirror, lines in his face entrenching themselves. What if the author's one of them, whaddayacallem, mulattos? One of those sterile hybrids begging for pack weight? The washed-up wunderkind, year out of a social work PhD, contract with the book company for a treatise on the state of America's children? His proposal had mentioned something like that. He couldn't remember. He burned it a long time ago.

Whatever it promised was due tomorrow.

He hadn't written a word before today. Things were working out nicely—every novel he'd ever attempted ended up seventeen pages long—this thing was fifty-nine easy and still running on its own steam.

Coming off a monthlong bender, he'd decided to go without sleep until he turned the book over—the deadline helped. He'd make up for the wasted time, the blizzard of blackouts, lost clothing, bent keys, ripped pants, shredded belts, the morning surprise of a deep skull cut, tucking in a piece of your brain.

He went downstairs to catch fresh air outside his building, watch his February breath, spit in the hedge. He was a jittering mess, cigarette burns along the insides of his fingers. Everything illuminated left trails. Palpitations, mini-seizures, auditory hallucinations.

An ancient black man with a canvas JFK handbag stood perfectly still in the vestibule; ex-president almost smiling, elbow on an absent desk, head still in one piece.

On the sidewalk a kid walked backwards, and a thug helped his grandma limp home.

Back in his room on television, a documentary about constrictors. The star crushed a rat in its coils. The rodent's nostrils popped snot bubbles. The snake brought its head around and stroked the victim's hair, took the head in its mouth, and slowly ingested the rest of the body.

Every other channel was clotted with crap. He accidentally watched QVC for twenty minutes, a sale on limited-edition porcelain Russian shell dolls, the kind you open and there's a slightly smaller replica inside it. You keep going until you reach the last one, microscopic and just as empty.

The next channel up had black-and-white footage of forties-era seaplanes, so he left it. Cameras in the bomb bay. Man shaking hands, smiling as he climbed from the cockpit. Sometimes on planes you hear, "Put your mask on first, then help others around you with their masks."

He'd heard some guy locked in the bathroom on speed wrote a novella in six hours. Didn't do him a lot of good though, since he couldn't tell you where to get methamphetamine this hour on Sunday. Monday, maybe. Besides, he shared a bathroom.

One memory he kept from the bender was he'd fallen and slashed his rib cage open. Not to the bone, but it got infected. Now he had to keep redressing it, pouring peroxide and leaning over the toilet, only to have the Band-Aids and medical tape end up in his pants five minutes later. He'd kept expanding on his bandages until he created the perfect gauze holster, wouldn't even move when you swung your arms around. He admired it in the mirror, thought, *Travis Bickel, M.D.*

He kept his windows open and between the noise of his fan and the traffic he always thought it was raining.

His phone never rang. Ever. It drove him crazy. Eventually he'd smash the cordless to bits, flush the wires and plastic pieces down the toilet. No one he could call anyway, even if his long distance was up and functional.

His mother hadn't answered her phone in five years. Who could it be? went her theory. Friends, relatives, creditors—they're all after the same thing: a piece of her. Every time the phone rings, someone's hungry for flesh. She said that before he moved out and she stopped taking calls.

"Is that like bells and angels?" he'd asked her.

But any humor'd leaked out of her bones long ago.

He couldn't tell you who or where his father was. His mother used to say things like "He's no longer with us," or "He's gone to a better place," but he never knew if that meant his dad was dead or evacuated to the suburbs. He'd stopped asking years ago. It got to seem childish, one of those, Why's the sky blue? What are those animals doing? Why do you fuck random guys while I'm in the next room? kind of questions.

His only friends whatever triumvirate of scumbags happened to be outside the corner deli. He did have three real friends in the city: one married, one with a baby, one K'd to the gills and skulking behind seven-lock doors down by White Street or somewhere on the outskirts of Vegas.

He headed outside again to smoke a cigarette, dump some trash, find whoever's drunk on the corner. There was the German intern from the borough paper and two others.

The intern said, "I am asking them, where in our news goes the accident report?"

A few glitter stickers of the Virgin Mary had been slapped against the deli Plexiglas, each one given a penis in permanent marker. After midnight you placed orders through a bullet-proof Lazy Susan. Black Gary wanted to know, from the sound of it, if it wasn't becoming the *Book of Children Victims,* or the *Victim's Book for Children.* BG wore an orange knit skullcap, like a piece of ski fence had blown loose and found his scalp.

The third guy was some shaky white trash who didn't say much, shivering shirtless in a vest, skin covered in blurry prison tattoos—crosses, names, acronyms, naked chick spread-eagle in a cocktail glass. When he did speak he told the story of a horrifying neon crucifix he saw off Times Square:

"Hands down drop dead worst thing I ever saw," the guy said.

Everyone agreed.

He watched the dirty full moon awhile, until he realized it was a streetlamp, thirteen feet from his face. Then he headed home.

Across the street a woman handed out religious flyers by the subway steps: Jesus DJing somewhere on the Lower East Side, $5 WITH INVITE. She had an incessant line of God babble she kept losing her place in, backtracking over four-word phrases like "He hath no time" and "The guilty shall not."

Down the subway staircase he could see underground lights and gum on the floor, two black cops, ripped and rearranged signs on the newly painted railings saying AIN'T WET and WET PAIN.

Most people are fortunate never to meet what breaks them.
Who said that? He couldn't remember.

He thought, for him, sure, it might've been the exgirlfriend, but it could just as easily have been his dad's cigarette ash flying into the backseat and burning his eye. Or watching his grandmother's casket close and having to lug it out of the church.

It didn't really matter what did it. He was here now. He'd been a mess for years and'd lost the ability to pretend he wasn't.

Back in the apartment he found the new roommate, yet another forty-year-old white guy half naked in front of the refrigerator with a six-pack and a side of roast beef in a Ziploc, blood pooling in a corner of the bag. He looked like a shirtless pregnant woman in threadbare cords.

"What're you gonna do with that?" he asked the new guy, pointing at the Ziploc.

"Drink it."

It was 3:30 by that point. He needed one last push to bump it over four hundred pages. He'd picked up a leftover Sunday *Times* from in front of someone's doorway. Foot-and-mouth had broken out in the UK and they were burning acres of cattle. They called it "contiguous culling," and a shortage of veterinarians was slowing down the killing. Farther down on the page: SUPREME COURT TO REVIEW EXECUTION OF RETARDED. He went out and sat on the fire escape. Came in and leaned on a wall. Saw he had cigarettes burning in three different ashtrays.

Somewhere in the past month he'd ripped a picture from a magazine and pinned it on the wall above his desk for inspiration: a photo of two lynched niggers and the crowd that came to witness. The caption said, AT THE HANDS OF UNKNOWN PARTIES, MARION, IND., AUG. 1930. The crowd all white, some in straw hats, girls holding up tiny pieces of clothing ripped off for souvenirs. One guy looking at the camera and pointing at the bodies, thinking, *See?* The caption also said the picture was so popular back in those days they made it into a postcard, five cents apiece.

He flew across cable channels: live traffic, team calf roping, explosions on the surface of the sun.

SEVENTEEN TEENAGERS DIE IN A BARN FIRE. TWELVE-YEAR-OLD FALLS OUT OF TREE. LACROSSE PLAYER HIT IN THE

HEART. PROSTITUTE IN THE RIVER. DAD BACKS OVER SON IN DRIVEWAY. CHILDREN TAKING OTHER CHILDREN OUT INTO FIELDS AND SLITTING THEIR THROATS.

He wrote for hours.

He woke up drooling on his printed-out manuscript at seven in the morning. He'd been scratching and crossing out and adding things in ink. The last thing he'd written in shaky capitals in the margin of page 247: YOUR STUFFED ANIMALS WILL ROT SLOWLY FROM THE INSIDE OUT.

He'd dreamt of third grade: left behind by the birthday bowling party minivan, friends waving out the back window. And another time, years later, smacked awake by his best friend's dad yelling, "You pulling a Japanese tourist on me?" Next thing he knew he was standing in the dead grass of D.C.'s quad lawn, surrounded by multiple Smithsonians. A fat black man in suspenders played the *CHiPs* theme on trumpet, just the first eight bars over and over.

The thing was due sometime this afternoon. So much for sorting. His wound ached in his armpit. He looked over what he'd written. Once the text wandered outside the U.S. he got lost. He'd never been to Africa, or Bosnia, or anywhere besides Hershey Park, the Grand Canyon, and Orlando.

What did he know about kids feigning death, lying on live grenades? Walking booby-trapped dogs. Squatting in a dark corner, machete in hand, waiting for their uncle.

On his television a fat, melancholy black woman ran through the standards, pretending she was happy. Caption read [*SOFT AND SUNNY SCAT SINGING.*]

Just before his first grad semester started, his mother said social work "don't help nobody cept folks can't help themselves to nothing but drugs or other people's TV sets."

He'd published a few articles making fun of America in the slickest men's magazines, magazines all about tits, kick-ass music, drinking games, explosions, race car wrecks, shit that makes you look cool. Guys ate them up with a pitchfork, bought five at a time of the same magazine, all with different names.

That in itself was enough to convince publishers he was hip on a spit and dripping juice. They'd taken him out to lunch at some place that served warden's portions. His possible future editor sucking on shrimp cocktail the size of a baby's arm.

He grabbed more paper.

Ten-year-old drug runner gunned down in cross fire. School bus runs over Brooklyn tot on second birthday. Drunk senior plowed his station wagon into the mall parking lot overpass, where now every Christmas they tie a ribbon. The preschooler whose skull has taken on a rock. Len Bias. Sitter loses her charge on a broken Ferris wheel. Newborn roasted on dashboard. Elementary schooler's electric wheelchair shorts in rush-hour intersection, mother says, "I thought we could make it across."

Page after page of teenage overdoses and alcohol poisoning.

Once, for his birthday, his ex-girlfriend gave him a dead moth in an orange prescription bottle. It was pink and yellow, dead and dry. She'd held the bottle over their heads, shook it.

"See," she said. "They don't live this far up north."

He asked what her point was.

"But it *died* here," she said.

He wrote that down and laid his head on the page.

Gigantic

AT THE ZOO I PARK BY BANGING MY AXLE AGAINST THE CURB and hope I can back the car out later. I have a laminated pass with my face and name on it which clips to my pocket and grants me a key to every cage.

I work at a University Thrift Zoo just outside Baltimore. We get secondhand animals from city zoos and "wildlife parks." There the rhinos and zebras get wide fields of dirt; all the cages are oversized, walls hand-painted to each natural habitat's specifications.

Here the cinder block is asylum manila and the animals lick the bars where thrown food smashed. Here we have a sluggish boa, digesting a tumor. Seals on climate-controlled plastic ice. We've got a tiger with green gums. This is where they put the retarded creatures and criminals—animals doing penance for something they committed when they were human.

Sign on the polar bears' open-air vivarium reads QUIET! BEARS SLEEPING! Kids hang on the rail, spit in the pool, wait for days to see bears that have long since been hauled away on flatbeds, under tarps, for burial out by the quarry.

The rhesus monkeys are property of the Psychology Department—all the primates are, actually—hair falling out, patches of pale pink skin, always throwing each other through tires or trying to rip their own ears off.

I rake dead bats from the hay floor of the bat cage and throw them in a black plastic bag. Later I'll take them to the dumpster and still no one'll be able to explain why the bats keep dropping like fruit, or why they have hay in a bat cage in the first place. I pick up a sign that says QUIET! _____ SLEEPING!, slip in the BATS panel, and place it up front, where all the kids can see it.

An hour till we open, I go see our one elephant, Clarice. She's already out and stamping through beige pebbles small as gallstones, testing her feet. When it rains she's kept caged for days—pacing the same figure eight, scraping the walls on her turns. Now she stands gigantic in the morning with a scab on her forehead thick as a tree trunk.

I blow through my lips, raise an arm, do a horrible impression of her species. She trumpets. We repeat this until she realizes I don't have food. She reaches beneath her feet, picks up a rock, and throws it to me. I put it in my pocket and blow her a kiss.

I walk back past the hippo in his dirty little bathtub to see Dewey digging a ditch behind the dumpsters.

"What died?" I say.

"This whole fucking zoo if you'd give it a minute. Place is a shit hole." Dewey's a white boy, sweating and powdered with dirt.

"Look what Clarice gave me."

"That a tooth?" Dewey says.

"It's a rock."

"Same thing."

The university owns this place, but Dewey's Uncle Don runs it, which means whenever Don wants to say anything he waits for the professor-of-the-day to come stick a hand up his ass and make him speak.

Dewey works here only in the summers, no official capacity; mostly walks around getting high and talking to the animals, occasionally burying whatever died last night. The rest of the year he's a terrible student at the university and smokes his entire allowance. He's got blond dreads with rings, beads, and seashells, greasy dandruff caught in the roots. First week I worked here, he said, "The moon might have cool booths and cheap drinks, but the earth's got *atmosphere*," and I've listened to less than half of what he's said ever since. That was two years ago.

"So what's dead now?" I say.

"D'you do those bats, Fiddy?" he asks me.

"They're right here," I say, holding up the bag I've still got with me.

"My dog," he says, points his shovel at the lumped beach towel next to his leg.

"He was sick."

"Not anymore."

Dewey's dog was a zoo favorite and free to wander the grounds; even Don didn't care. It was a bull terrier that smiled when it panted and made kids laugh— they'd pet him, giggle, drop ice cream and french fries on his back. Never once barked or so much as growled. The thing had been skinny to begin with, but for a while now would throw up everything it ate, right on the zoo path, staggering through the crowds. Wasting away right in front of us, nothing we could do about it. Wasn't like the dog didn't eat. We'd catch him in the dumpsters at least twice a day, pull him out by the collar, Dewey smacking his ass with that same shovel.

"I can't believe Brutus is dead."

"Brewster," he says.

"Isn't that what I said?"

Dewey rubs his forehead and stares at the dirt paste in his hand.

"Well, I still can't believe he's dead," I say.

"Believe it," he says. "You can check for yourself." He pokes the towel a couple times and we wait for it to move. "See?"

"I see a hole without a dog," Uncle Don says, appearing suddenly among us in a baby-blue sweatsuit, fat and slightly mafioso. His hair's Grecian, curly and kelplike. He's shiny. Olive oil for sunblock. "I see two thumbs in two asses and everybody wondering where their hands went."

Dewey kicks the corpse and towel into the hole. It takes a few tries.

"What's in the bag?" Don asks me.

"Cafeteria trash," I say.

"Then why's it moving?"

"Goddamn rats," I say, drop the bag to the ground and step on the part that's still squirming.

Don holds up his hands like he just bought them. He says, "One of the psych freaks told me they found pot plants in the gorilla compound."

Dewey stops throwing dirt with the ditch half-filled. Puts his foot on the shovel blade and says, "They?"

I say, "Compound?"

"You ever heard of gorillas?" Don says. "Know where we keep 'em? Well. In there. The only people with keys besides me and the psych department is you two."

"And . . . ," Dewey says.

"So . . . ," Don says.

"Wasn't me," I say.

"I haven't accused anybody yet."

But Dewey and I have, sneering at each other like we're losing charades. "Maybe it just grew wild," Dewey says. "Maybe they brought seeds over in their fur. Like bees, maybe."

Don says, "It had an electric fence around it."

Dewey points the shovel at me. "Then Fiddy did it."

"He called your zoo a shit hole," I say.

Dewey looks at his uncle and wants to know who he's gonna believe, but Don's staring right at me. "What'll the psychology people think?" he wants to know, furious with his pulse in his face.

Fired from the zoo at two in the afternoon and now I have nothing to do. I head for a bar in the city. I just called Max, someone I know who'll drink during daylight hours. Most people drink until they're twenty-five; some ride it out to thirty. The rest of us turn pro. I'm having a terrible year and the fans are against me.

I smoke outside the bar, flick sparks on passing dogs behind their walkers' backs. Trees unfold from mulch under sewer grates. I'm feeling sorry for myself, stench like a kennel, when up walks Max: sag-eyed white kid, skinny as a cartoon chicken singing Bing Crosby. There's blood on his T-shirt; on his neck six inches of insect-black stitches. "Just ran into the woman I love," he says.

"That how you got that gash?" I say.

"In a way, I mean, I was walking around staring at the hooks in the ceiling of the tire warehouse where I'm temping—yeah, I don't know, that's why I'm staring—and I come out from one of those four-story pallet alleys and I fucking drill her. Not literally or nothing like that, just ran right into her and knocked off her hard hat. I'm holding her arms so she won't fall, you know, 'cause women like that sort of thing, I mean, I had her *elbows* in my *hands* and I say—wait, what'd I say, oh yeah—I say, 'Excuse me,' and this forklift swings around almost lops my head off."

"What'd she say?"

"Couldn't hear her. 'Cause of the forklift." We both squint downstreet at heat rising out of the sidewalk.

He and I always have these stories. Finally get introduced to a girl and puke under the table. Or she disappears into the parking lot with her ex-boyfriend, half an hour into your first date. "Maybe you didn't miss anything," I say. "Maybe she didn't even open her mouth."

He stretches his neck so you can see the thread pulling on the skin. He says, "It's worse than it looks. I mean better." He's got on surgeon-green pants he stole from Emergency. "These aren't even mine," he says, and he might mean the pants or the blood spots.

Max and I are friends because we're afraid to drink alone. In public, anyway. We're like a guy and his CPR dummy so he can drive in the carpool lane. We alternate roles.

In the bar, when the door shuts, it takes at least a minute to see shapes. Another minute to see the whole place: a salmon cinder-block pit with no windows; every inch of wall holds a beer mirror and it's smoky even when it's empty.

Or almost empty. Albert the resident regular sits at the rail end in his fedora, newspaper-gray skin, drinking Jack and Tabs and stabbing empty soda cans with a pen. Smoke coming from the neck of his ancient suit.

Max says, "Hey Albert, you dead yet?"

Albert points a two-finger pistol with a lit cigarette in its tips, says in a voice you could sharpen rocks with, "What's with the neck, Frankenstein. You kill somebody?"

"Forklift at that place I was temping. You know how it is."

"Lucky it ain't cut your juggler."

"Plus I got a pair of pants."

I pull out money, say, "You probably want another one, don't you Albert?"

"Don't lecture me, motherfucker."

Rufus the bartender is big enough to count as a couple in the census and black as his weight in coffee beans. He's got the floor raised so he can roll in front of the liquor on a three-wheel stool. He shifts his mass in his yellow windbreaker like a rhino trapped in a tent. He's on the phone. "I'm on the phone," he says to us. On television they've got tarps on the Kansas City infield; players sit in dugouts and spit through the rain.

Rufus sets the phone down, announces, "I'm having a kid!" Arms up like touchdown.

"No you're not, you're just fat. Now bring us some drinks," Max says.

"Hey Fiddy," Rufus says to me. "Why you always hang out with white boys?"

I shrug.

Rufus says, "Betchugotta cracker bitch too."

"I'm bitchless."

"Betchu," Rufus says. Hand up his jacket, rubbing sweat from under one of his breasts.

Max thinks he's a poet. He sets his manuscript on the bar, cover page tie-dyed by food stains. Title: "Midget's in My Attic." "I'm thinking about taking out the apostrophe," he says.

"You should leave it," I say.

He flips to a page near the back. "Read this one," he says. He's got his hand in my shirt pocket, wrestling a pack of cigarettes. "Hey Rufus, you here again?" he says. "You're a goddamn workaholic."

"What's that make you," Rufus says.

"My point exactly."

The poem's called "Smelt Night." The first line: *Cheap wine always brings the roaches out of hiding.*

Rufus stares at the television, rolls in the back of his neck like a pack of black hot dogs. He says, "So seriously guys, Gina's having a baby."

"Well why the hell didn't you say so in the first place!" Max says. "You *know* what this calls for, Rufus. A celebration. Shots around the bar! All—wait—one, two, four of us! Hook it up, my man. And that's countin you, señor, so make yourself one while you're at it."

"Thanks for permission," Rufus says. He gives us sewage-beige shots spilling from rocks glasses.

"To the soon-to-be father!" Max stands on his stool now. "Please, God, let it be a girl!" and we all scream, even Rufus. Max downs his glass, shudders and winces, puts his head in his arms, and doesn't talk for a few minutes. My friend the manual-labor temp. He'd work the worst shifts you ever heard of, then take a week off to drink.

I'd actually liked my job. On good days I felt like I was keeping the animals alive, even if only for another week, before they got chucked in the dumpster or loaded onto trucks by crane.

I pull the rock from my pocket, turn it over in my fingers. It's perfectly smooth and the size of a miniature ear. First thing an animal ever gave me that didn't leave a scar. I'll miss Clarice. She made my mornings, shaking her head in the sun. That's why I liked that place: this rock, her enormous head. The tiger on its back, tongue out, letting me hose the dirt off its belly. I should've brought Clarice birthday cakes every day, hand-fed her gourmet lettuce.

Then I remember her lying on her side, wailing in her cage, and think maybe I should have mercy-killed her before I left. Should've done the monkeys, too, for that matter. I'd need a giant blade—a scimitar maybe, machete even, some one-stroke stuff—gas pellets in the ventilation shafts, poisonous vegetables.

I had promised myself one cigarette per drink, but

after a few doubles the world sped up and by now I had two cigarettes left in what had been a fresh pack and I'd lost count of my drinks. I'd tipped Rufus obscenely and he'd yet to throw me a buy-back.

Max is up again and yammering next to me. "I don't care," he says to Albert. "Just don't give me a job where every day I might die. Like the president. Or a stewardess."

Albert says, "Yeah. What else?"

"Keeping busy," Max says. "Trying to juggle two chicks at once."

"Two?"

"At the same time."

Albert says, "That ain't juggling, man. You're just passing your balls from hand to hand."

On TV the rain delay's over; a player tomahawks a bat at the kid who collects them; bleacher people throw food in the bull pen.

Bar's suddenly packed for happy hour, two blocks from Camden Yards and the Orioles have a game at seven. Rufus sliding like a maniac, sparks on his wheels.

The place crowded now to the point of freakish: people hanging from the rafters, popping out of one another's backs, growing from puddles on the bar.

"How long we been here," I ask nobody.

"Three hours," they answer.

Through the suits and smoke Dewey comes through the door, still in his zoo jumpsuit. He grabs the stool next to me—him on one side, a nearly passed out Max on the other, me staring at three shelves of liquor posing for their all-star photo.

Dewey says, "Dude." I take this to mean he's speaking seriously. "I feel superbad about what happened."

"Who the fuck is this guy?" Max asks. "Hey. Hey you. Nice hair. Close your eyes before you bleed to death." He's standing next to me, eagerly spinning his barstool like a kid's riding on it. Much as I despise Max sometimes, he and I are soul mates compared to anything I feel for Dewey.

"I didn't know my uncle'd fire you, Fiddy," Dewey says. "I so had no idea."

"D'you think about what he *might* do?" I say.

He thinks about it, says, "I'll admit I never got that far."

Max wipes whiskey on twenties and wallpapers his forehead.

Behind me someone screams, "Hey barkeep that's the fourth dolla ya fuckin jukebox tooka mine!"

Rufus says, "Then stop putting money in it!"

Dewey gives me a shark tooth on a leather shoelace and a Buddhist prayer bracelet with mood beads. He's been quiet and slightly weepy, and now with the gifts it feels like a breakup. If I'd just take them it'd make him feel better. He says he'll buy me a drink.

I point to the drink I have, push it over on the bar. "Second thought, I will take one. Him too." The stool next to me empty, Max in back screaming at the pay phone.

"What's he drink?" Dewey says.

"Wet stuff. Not a lot of ice."

Dewey keeps staring at his hands on his knees, like he just heard his dog died. He says, "I didn't mean," and "But I just."

"You just. Just came all the way down here to give me beads, that's what you just."

"And a shark tooth. And to get your badge."

"Point being: fuck you very much, Dewey, I don't want the shark tooth. I found it by the food court and gave it to you. If I wanted it, I'da kept it."

Max spilled his last drink too, so when he comes back and sits down he leaves his on the bar, leans over and takes it from the straw. The prayer beads are going from black to bloodred to deep sea green, right there against my glass.

"I'll take these beads though," I say.

"I found those," Dewey says.

"Your girlfriend gave you this bracelet. I was there."

"They change color according to your karma."

"That's exactly what she said," I say.

"So, your badge."

"I'm what?"

"Your pass," he says. "That little thing lets you in the zoo every morning. I need it back."

"My pass . . . ," I say, so slowly I hope he leaves before I finish. I tried to burn my pass earlier, but the lamination stank so much I gave up. Now it's curled in my pocket, black-brown and half the size it used to be.

Dewey still sits there. Everyone else in the bar races their drinks to their faces, glancing side-eyed like in a pie-eating contest.

"Here it is," I say, hold it up hidden in my fist, accidentally throw it on the floor on purpose. I say to his back as he's bent over, "Anyway, my friend and I were just leaving."

Max says, "Who. Me?"

We head home in silence. I have drunk, concentric thoughts and serious trouble with gravity. Max so loaded he walks like his shoulder's separated. We take to a curb in the Camden Yards parking lot; watch minivans wander the aisles, late for the game. Even from here you can see bugs cloud the stadium floodlights and listen to the loud hollow crowd noise like a riot in a tunnel.

A cop rolls up so slow I start thinking detox, stand slightly more sober for an instant. The squad stops in front of us. I salute.

"Your friend okay?" cop says.

"He's tired," I say. "He got fired. Hey that rhymed."

"Poet and you didn't know it."

"But my feet show it 'cause they're long fellers."

The cop produces an arm from the car window and in the hand on the end of his ham of a forearm he holds two paper squares. Rectangles maybe. "Want tickets there, pally? Six-buck special. For the salute."

"All I got's a twenty."

He gives me the tickets, takes the twenty. Drives away instead of making change.

I kick Max's legs, try to lift him by his torso. "Tickets, man! Tick-ets!"

"Go on without me," he says, picking at his stitches. "I'm not gonna make it."

"Don't you die on me now. We're almost at the chopper."

Eventually I get him to his feet, arm over my shoulder. "Gimme a minute," he says. He lurches up against a tree trunk and violently dry heaves for a while. When he's done he puts his hands on his knees and spits in the grass. Takes a deep breath.

"There you go," I say. "In with the good stuff, out with the bad."

He arches his back, spreads his fists, and howls at the moon, "O REE OOOOOOOOOS!" Smiles at me with his eyes closed, swaying. "Okay, I'm ready. Wait—" Stops smiling. "News flash." He pukes on the curb, his shirt, his ER scrubs; paints a station wagon; fills the back of a pickup; finally falls on his back in the grass, breathing like a sedated beast.

I poke his head with my toe. "Maybe I will go on without you." I crouch and slap him—repeatedly. "Hey," I say. "Hey," again and again and again in time with each slap. It's kind of fun. Nothing will move him. "Well," I tell the tree, "I tried." The tree understands. "Stay here, Max." I fold a ticket and set it on his nose.

From the stadium speakers someone screams how they got their mojo working. The gate lady waves me through without ripping my ticket. As I'm headed for my section the music cuts off. The crowd starts in, louder than ever, like they're getting their limbs torn off, but no, they're chanting somebody's name—it's my name—the whole of Camden Yards chanting, "FIH DY! FIH DY! FIH DY!" I come from the tunnel into fists and faces and foam fingers waving and across the field on the Sony Jumbotron I see a two-story picture of some guy named Eddie and none of this has anything to do with me.

I don't remember how the game was, or who won. I remember fat red people wrestling. A guy in a rainbow wig with someone's name and time of day on cardboard: "John 3:16." I wanted to tell him, "It's almost ten. John's not coming."

At one point the big screen said,

JASON SCHENKBERG
IN SECTION 113 SAYS:
PAULA,
WILL YOU MARRY ME?

It showed the couple in their seats. She seemed stunned, eyes still on the Jumbotron while he sat with a beer and the ring in his hands. She winced, leaned away, slid in her finger like she was reaching in the garbage. He kissed her and spilled beer on her pants. The guy behind them gave them a ball—a foul tip he'd caught earlier, when the PA'd screamed, "Give that fan a contract!"

Next thing the game's over; people headed for the exits, mooing, laughing, pushing each other into strangers. I'm outside the stadium in the gigantic blue night, scab of a moon on its forehead.

I find Max facedown in the median grass, sleeping like he fell off a building. A bucktoothed black kid with walleye squats, pokes the back of Max's neck. "Your friend okay?" he wants to know.

"He ate something funny."

"He ain't laughing."

Around us the crowd spreads toward their cars. Somewhere someone screams, "Nimrod! Get your black ass back over heuh!" Nimrod laughing through his fingers, hiding his enormous teeth. He keeps the wandering eye on me.

I have to squint to get him in focus. Closing one eye helps. The kid's got my prayer beads—big as a belt on his wrist, fingers spread wide so they won't fall off. I'd stretched them over top a fire hydrant when we first sat on the curb. "Where'd you get those?"

"They're mine."

"Nimrod!" His massive mother comes from the rows of cars, stands legs spread with her fists on her waist. "Boy, don't make me come over there."

"We're just talking, ma'am," I say.

"Ain't nobody ask yo drunk ass."

"True enough."

She turns away from us and lumbers back from where she came, says over her shoulder, "Nimrod, you don't beat me to the car, I'ma whoop you shiny."

He gets halfway to the car when I say, "Hey, kid," like Mean Joe Green in the Coke commercial. I reach in my shirt. Throw him the rock and he puts it in his pocket.

ACKNOWLEDGMENTS

For the heavy lifting and demolition work they contributed toward the completion of this book I'd like to thank the following: Amy Williams, my dear friend and agent who deserves a place in the Justice League for her omnipotence and flying abilities; my editor, Brendan Cahill, whose patience, skill, credit card, and extra-wide red pen were invaluable; and lastly, the big man, Elwood Reid, who has always had my back, helped me out from the moment we first met, and is truly a saint in the form of a lumberjack.